Murder in t

Lionel Trevor/Tech Squad Mysteries

Harold Emanuel

Table of Contents

MURDER AT THE PLAYHOUSE

Let me introduce myself. My name is Lionel Trevor, Professor Lionel Trevor, although my students usually just call me Doc, or Prof. I lead a Forensic Technology workshop at Tampa Bay Community College. I picked five of my best students to be part of this workshop in conjunction with the local Sheriff's Department. The program was meant to be a learning experience for participants but has proven to be much more. As my friend of over forty years, Sheriff Tony Maggio, explained, "the county spent beaucoup bucks to buy all that techy equipment, but our guys have been slow to accept it. They still like to investigate crimes the old-fashioned way, using shoe leather, note pads, and pencils. Your kids understand technology and need to learn about criminal investigation. The combination of our police know-how and your students' computer savvy can go a long way to closing cases."

The students named their group The Tech Squad. They have already helped the sheriff solve a murder case. I had a front row seat to most of this story and I found out the rest by— Well, you'll see. Let me tell you what happened.

* * *

Rita Diaz knew this day would come and she dreaded it. She's sitting in the Southshore Nursing Home office, completing the paperwork to have her mother moved to the funeral home in preparation for burial. The facility's staff had done an excellent job decorating for Christmas, but Rita is not in a festive mood. She's afraid she will now always associate the holiday with her mother's death.

1

Emanuel

Rita is a striking woman, tall, with short, jet black hair and deep blue eyes who, at age 55, can still turn men's heads as they pass her on the street.

"For most of the three months she lived here she didn't even know my name, but her death is still hard to accept," Rita says. "Since my father died, it's just been mom and me. Now it's just me."

Dr. Soloff and Adiva Fayed, a college student volunteer, sit with Rita, guiding her as the grieving daughter completes the required forms.

"Before she died, she kept asking for Hope," Adiva says. "That name is not on the list of visitors. Do you know who she is? Should we contact her?"

A tear rolls down Rita's cheek. "Hope is—was my older sister. She died almost forty years ago. Although mom never said so, I think Hope was her favorite. She was pretty and smart. She even won a scholarship to Florida West Coast University. Forty-five years ago, it wasn't easy for a girl to get a scholarship, in engineering, no less. After all, it was the man's job to earn a living and support a family. Girls didn't need an education, but Hope bucked the trend. Mom was so disappointed when she dropped out during her sophomore year after — Anyway, that was a long time ago."

Dr. Soloff sees the sadness in Rita's face. She wants to cheer her up. "Your mother must have been proud of you when you went to college, earned advanced degrees, and now have a career as a professor at Tampa Bay Community College. I think you said your field is botany. Is that right?"

Rita's face brightens. "She was proud of me, but Hope was special. My sister's death left a hole in both of our hearts that never healed."

Rita completes the paperwork and heads toward her car. As she drives home, she tells herself that her mother is in a better place. She was a proud woman who wouldn't want to live in a nursing home, not remembering her own

2

daughter. Rita pulls into her driveway, turns off the motor, and begins to sob. She fingers the initial pendant she wears. When she and Hope were growing up her mother made them matching jewelry. As a teenager, her wealthier classmates made fun of her *cheap junk*, but she didn't care. Her mother made the necklaces, bracelets, and brooches. Rita knew that her big sister, who she adored, wore the same jewelry. Her mother stopped making it when Hope died. Although the two women never talked about it, they both knew; Hope's suicide was his fault.

* * *

It's a mild late March afternoon, one of the few days in Florida when you can turn off the air conditioner and open a window. Professor Donald Devries and I are sitting in the faculty lounge, enjoying a cup of coffee, when the door opens, and Professor Rita Diaz enters. I see Donald's eyes follow the attractive Botany professor as she walks toward the Keurig coffee maker.

"Well, if it isn't my two favorite colleagues, Ichabod and the aging hippie," she says, smiling.

Some of the Tampa Bay Community College faculty gave me the nickname *Ichabod*. I'm just over six feet tall and weigh no more than one hundred and fifty-five pounds. They say I look like *Ichabod Crane*, referring to Washington Irving's *The Legend of Sleepy Hollow* character. I don't mind the comparison. My wife tells me she finds my protruding Adam's apple sexy. That's enough for me.

Professor Devries is a half a foot shorter than me, stocky, with a receding hairline, and a ponytail that hangs to his shoulders. He once told me he grew the ponytail during his undergraduate days, when it was fashionable, and never cut it off. He admits it may look out of place on a 56-year-old man, but he doesn't care. He likes the pony tail.

Emanuel

"I was surprised to see you back when the semester began in January, so soon after your mother's death," Donald says.

Rita prepares a cup of decaf. "She wouldn't have wanted me to take time away from my students. She had to drop out of school after the eighth grade to help support her family but was determined to get her high school diploma, which she did at age forty-nine. Education was very important to her. Thanks for thinking about her. On another topic, do you have your lines down yet?"

"Just about," Donald replies, "except for that long speech I have in the second act. Performing in community theater seemed like a good idea when I first auditioned, but who would have guessed I'd land such a big part. You're lucky. What do you have, maybe ten lines?"

"Eight," Rita answers, "but they're difficult lines. Some even have multi-syllabic words. And Lionel, you have the best role of all?"

"You're right, I don't have a speaking part. I just come on stage, place the beer on the table, and leave. I also work behind the scenes, helping the stage manager."

"I wish I had your role," Donald offers. "I've spent at least two hours every night for the past two weeks memorizing my part and I still mess up."

Rita pulls a chair up next to Donald. "Tell you what, Don, I'll read lines with you. That should help you learn them."

"I'd appreciate the help."

"There is a price. I'm taking my class on a field trip next Tuesday. It's difficult for one professor to keep track of twenty-seven students. I could use a second chaperone."

Donald doesn't have to be coaxed. "I'll be there."

"Great. If you have a few minutes, could you walk with me to the Botany lab? I'll show you what we will be doing on the field trip. Do you want to join us, Lionel?"

Murder At The Playhouse

I think about volunteering to help chaperone the field trip but decide against it. I suspect the shy Donald is looking for an opportunity to get to know Rita better. I also notice Rita fingering the initial pendant she wears around her neck. I suspect it might be a nervous habit. Maybe she's as interested in Donald as he is in her. A third person would just be in the way. "I'll pass but, don't forget, I'll be with you in cyberspace."

"Yes, you will," Rita says, "and we appreciate your efforts."

I can tell by the puzzled look on Donald's face that he doesn't understand my comment about seeing Rita in cyberspace. He will.

After finishing our coffee, the three of us leave the faculty lounge. I head toward my office while Rita and Donald go to the Botany lab.

* * *

"You know, Don," Rita says as they walk across campus, "one of our play's cast members really gets on my nerves, that asshole, Billy Agnew. He's such an arrogant prick. There's something about him that just annoys the hell out of me. I don't know what it is."

Donald is taken aback that the refined Rita Diaz uses such language, but he understands why. "Agnew lives three houses down from me in Sun Coast Shores. I feel my blood pressure spike every time I see him."

"What did he do to you?"

"It wasn't to me. It's my daughter. She lives in Atlanta and used to visit at least once a month after my wife died. She knew how lonely I was, but that SOB Agnew wouldn't leave her alone. He'd comment on her looks when she went for a walk or a swim in the pool. Now, when I want to see her, I have to go to Atlanta."

"Did you contact the police or your community security force?"

5

Emanuel

"I did, but they both said being a disgusting lecher isn't against the law or the community bylaws. If I had known he'd be in the show, I'd never have auditioned. He's taken the fun out of it. There are times I wish he was dead."

"Keep your chin up," Rita says, gently placing her hand on Donald's chin. "It's only two weeks and the show will be behind us."

"I don't understand why he ever auditioned for the play," Donald replies. "He doesn't strike me as the community theater actor type."

"I think he's trying to please his wife."

"She's a nutritionist, isn't she? I think she'll be speaking at a meeting of my community association next week."

"She teaches the Nutrition Technician Certificate program at the college. She'll be helping my students analyze the nutritional value of some of the plants they gather on our field trip."

The two professors enter the Botany lab and sit at one of the tables. Donald notices floor to ceiling shelves containing plants of all types. The fragrance of the fauna throughout the room fills his nostrils. It's a much more pleasing scent than he experiences in his own chemistry lab. Rita shows Donald the plants they expect to see. Her students will be collecting them to take back to the lab for further analysis. They then discuss the logistics of the field trip.

It's 5:30 when they finish their planning session. Donald sees his chance. "Getting hungry?"

"I am," Rita replies, fingering her pendant.

"Ever been to Giovani's? Best Italian restaurant in the area. We can grab some pasta before the rehearsal. I know Tom Woodson, the manager. It's just down the road."

"I've never been there. I'd love to go."

Donald pauses for a moment. "Can I ask you a personal question?"

6

"Sure."

"I notice that pendant you always wear. It's attractive and it looks hand-made. My wife used to make jewelry and I can usually tell the difference between hand-made and manufactured, store-bought, jewelry."

"You're right," Rita says. "My mother made it."

"I notice that the initial is 'M' but your name is Rita. Why do you wear an 'M' pendant? Was that your mother's initial?"

"No, it's because my given name is Margarita. When I was in college the craze was for people with ethnic sounding names to make them more American, so I decided to call myself Rita. Today, many young people want to be known by ethnic names. I have a student in one of my classes, Christopher Sanchez, who has legally changed his name to Carlos. I think this trend's a good thing."

"I agree," Donald replies. As the two leave the Botany lab and walk toward the school parking lot, Donald takes Rita's hand. The Botany professor doesn't resist.

* * *

Rita catches the faint aroma of Italian herbs and spices as she and Donald approach the restaurant.

"Welcome back to Giovani's, Professor Devries." Tom has managed this exclusive Italian restaurant for over 15 years and has gotten to know his regular customers. He remembers that Donald's wife died over a year ago. Since then he has been here many times with friends and sometimes by himself. This is the first time he has come with a woman. *This is a good sign,* he thinks. *Maybe the professor's beginning to spread his wings.*

"Thanks, Tom. I don't have a reservation. Do you have a table overlooking the bay?"

The restaurant manager opens his iPad to check the reservations for the evening. "Right this way. Mary will be taking care of you."

Emanuel

Over the years Tom has learned to show a happy face to customers even if he's feeling stressed. The cause of this stress is sitting in his office.

"For Christ sake, Benito," Tom says, slamming the door to his office and staring at the man sitting in the chair next to his desk, "we can't use your suppliers. Our customers are used to the finest ingredients in their food. We've sampled the stuff your guys from— Where are they from again, Mexico? It's inferior."

"It's also cheaper." Benito Delgado is used to hearing this from restaurant managers. As Regional Coordinator for CGI International he's the front man when his company purchases a local independent restaurant. His job is to squeeze as much profit as possible, as quickly as possible. His bonuses depend on his getting results and his three ex-wives and five kids depend on these bonuses.

"Come on, Tim."

"It's Tom."

"OK, Tom, your customers won't know the difference. Anyway, you don't have a choice. CGI owns, what's it called, Gene something?"

"Giovani's."

"Whatever. You either use our suppliers or we'll find a restaurant manager who will. Cancel your contracts with your suppliers. You'll receive the first shipment from the new guys in five days."

"Five days, that's impossible! Whenever I use a new supplier from outside the country, I have to file with both the U.S. Food and Drug Administration and the Florida Department of Health. The approval process takes at least a month and then each shipment has to be inspected."

Benito just stares at the restaurant manager. *This guy doesn't understand how CGI handles those asshole inspectors*, he thinks. *He'll learn.* "As I said, you'll receive your first shipment in five days."

* * *

8

The evening's rehearsal is almost over. Donald and Rita kept their eyes on each other throughout the play. I guess I was right to leave them alone this afternoon. I'm helping the sound engineer ensure that the microphones are working properly. Billy Agnew and Laura Cannon are just finishing the final scene before the curtain falls. Our school's art department had worked with theater volunteers to create a set representing the front porch of a 1940s mid-western farmhouse. A local lumber yard had donated the wood for a rail fence and an antique store had loaned us a rocking chair and table from that period.

"Dad," Laura says, attempting to take a bottle from Billy's hand, "you can't keep drinking those beers. That's your third this afternoon. You remember what the doctor said."

"Ah, what do them damn doctors know?" Billy responds, pulling his arm toward his body so Laura can't grab his drink. "My father, your grandfather, gave me my first beer when I was twelve. Some of my best memories with him were when he and me were sittin' on the porch after dinner, drinkin'."

"Yeah, and grandpa died of cirrhosis of the liver when he was sixty-one," Laura says. "You're almost sixty. We'd like to have you around for a little while longer."

"Don't worry, honey," Billy replies, gently touching Laura's face, "I'll be around for a good, long time. I want to see that little fella of yours grow up, get married, and give me some great grandkids."

Billy takes one last sip of beer, throws his arms up, tosses the bottle across the stage, tips his chair backwards and falls.

"No!" Stuart Abbott shouts, storming up the stairs to the stage and confronting Billy. Everyone sees the frustration on the director's face. Stuart had been a professional actor on Broadway and in traveling companies throughout the world. He's proud of telling

Emanuel

everyone who will listen how he once played opposite
Dame Regina Wentworth in performances in London's
Globe theater. Stuart's retired now and living in Sun
Coast Shores. Stuart and Laura, a retired high school
English teacher, were instrumental in creating the Sun
Coast Shores Community Theater. "Billy, how many
times have I told you, after you take that last sip of beer
your head falls to your chest and you die, quietly. That's
the way the play ends. You don't flail around like a fish
out of water."

"Yeah," Billy replies, "but I figure I should put some
action into it."

The rest of the cast sees the veins in Stuart's neck
bulge. "Who am I?" Stuart asks.

"Stuart."

"And what's my role in this production?"

"You're the director."

"Exactly. Now, let's try it again and this time take a sip
of the beer and let your head drop to your chest."

Billy glares at Stuart. I could see that his alpha male
personality hates taking direction from anyone, especially
an 80-year-old former actor. I understand why. After one
rehearsal, I invited Billy to stop for a beer. I knew what
Donald and Rita thought about him. I wanted to see for
myself. After two beers Billy opened up. "Real men aren't
actors," he told me. "Real men run construction
companies, like I did. I'm only in this play because my
dumb-ass wife insisted. I know why I married someone
30 years my junior, with a body like that. I didn't realize
what I would have to do to get what I want from her." I
now know why Donald and Rita feel the way they do
about Billy. I agree with them.

Stuart returns to his seat in the theater's front row.
"OK, Billy, repeat your last line again and then die like I
told you."

Billy and Laura take their positions on stage. "Don't
worry, honey," Billy says, "I'll be around for a good, long

10

time. I want to see that little fella of yours grow up, get married and give me some great grandkids."

Everyone's eyes are on Billy as he takes one last sip of beer and drops his head to his chest.

"Excellent," Stuart says. "Now, let's see if you can remember to play the scene that way for the remainder of the rehearsals and during the performances. Do you think you can do that, Billy?"

Billy does not answer. He just glares at the director.

Ellen Agnew, Billy's wife, is sitting in the back of the theater during the rehearsal, waiting for her husband. Ellen has a small part in the play but is not in the scenes being rehearsed that evening. "You were great, honey. How about we go out for pizza? We can even get extra mushrooms. I know you like mushrooms and the restaurant down the roads knows that you like yours piping hot. You won't have to return the pizza to be re-heated, like you do when you receive it cold."

"Nah," Billy says, "I'm meeting with some of the boys for a beer. When I'm with these guys I don't have to listen to that stupid girl talk I get from you. I'm sure someone can give you a lift." Billy leaves the theater without waiting to see who will take Ellen home.

Rita Diaz puts her arm around Ellen's shoulder and sees the anguished expression on the younger woman's face and the tears welling up in her eyes. "I'll take you home," she says.

"Billy's usually real nice to me," Ellen replies, "but sometimes he's not."

* * *

The two women drive the four miles to the Agnew home. Ellen sits quietly in the passenger seat, her arms folded over her chest and her legs curled under her. Rita recognizes the posture of a woman who has been beaten down, if not physically, then emotionally. It confirms her opinion of Billy Agnew. He's a jerk.

Emanuel

"Would you like to come in for a cup of coffee?" Ellen asks, as they pull into her driveway. Rita is tired from a busy day at school and the rehearsal, but she senses that Rita wants to talk.

"I'd love to."

As Ellen prepares the coffee, Rita sits on the overstuffed family room couch. Looking around, she sees that the Agnew home is just one large man-cave, filled with heavy furniture, pictures of wild animals, and scantily clothed women and what appears to be football trophies. There is little of the female touch in the home's decor.

Ellen places the tray with the coffee pot, cups, cream and sweetener, on the table in front of the couch. "When I was younger, I had this fantasy of being an actress," Ellen says. "I performed when I was in college. I guess that's why I asked Billy to be in this play. It's something we could do together, but I don't think he's enjoying it. He's really a nice guy, you know, and generous. He gave me this necklace and pendant when we got engaged." Ellen fingers the pendant. "See, it's my initial on a chain. He said he had it made just for me. I knew then that he really loved me. He didn't just buy any pendant. He had one made."

"That's an interesting piece of jewelry." Rita lets her gaze rest on the initial on the chain around Ellen's neck. She decides to change the subject. "How did you meet Billy?"

"We met in my senior year in college. He ran this construction company that was doing work on campus. I was having lunch in the school cafeteria. He and two of his crew sat near me and one of them made some crude remarks. I was only twenty-one and didn't know how to handle older men. Billy stepped in and told the man to apologize. He was my knight in shining armor or, in this case, a tee shirt and work boots. He was so big and strong. He had played football at some college, you know.

It was a local school, somewhere near Tampa. The next day Billy saw me, asked how I was and said he wanted to take me to dinner. He proposed six months later."

The two women finish their coffee and Rita gets up to leave. "I appreciate your bringing me home and coming in," Ellen says as she picks up her phone. "Would you mind if I took a selfie of the two of us? I like to have pictures of my friends."

"Of course."

The two women stand with their heads close together and Ellen snaps a picture.

"I'll send you a copy," Ellen says.

"Thanks, and I also want to thank you for volunteering your class to help my students evaluate the nutritional value of the edible plants they collect on our field trip." Rita responds.

"I'm glad I can help."

As Rita walks toward the door she turns and glances back at Ellen. Now she knows why she feels as she does about Billy Agnew.

* * *

Ellen Agnew glances at her notes as she stands behind the podium at the Sun Coast Shores Community meeting. "So, let's summarize. As we age, our metabolism slows down so we have to be extra careful about what we eat so we can stay healthy."

Billy Agnew, sitting in a folding chair in the third row, smiles and looks around at his neighbors. He suspects why most of the men in the audience came to this meeting. They have no interest in his wife's nutrition presentation. They came to see her. At five feet, ten inches tall, with her long auburn hair, coal black eyes and those legs that won't quit, he imagines he's the envy of every man in the room. "She's obviously eating healthy. She still has the same hot body she had when I married her," he says, in a whisper loud enough for those around him to hear. He loves seeing his neighbors' reactions when he says something they think to be inappropriate. Donald Devries is sitting three chairs over from Billy. "Hey, Don," Billy continues, in that same loud whisper, "when is that daughter of yours coming back to visit? I'd love to see her at the pool in that bikini again."

Donald is about to jump out of his chair and take a swing at Billy but thinks better of it. Billy outweighs Donald by a good fifty pounds, all of it muscle. He'll have to find another way to get back at that son-of-a-bitch.

Ellen stiffens as she stands at the podium. She's heard Billy's comments. His rudeness, especially in public, is becoming more than she can take.

Morris Greenberg, President of the Sun Coast Shores Community Association, steps to the podium. "Does anyone have any questions for Mrs. Agnew?" he asks. After about 10 seconds of silence he assumes there are no questions. "Thank you, Mrs. Agnew, for that excellent presentation."

As Ellen leaves the podium Billy grabs her arm. "Come on, babe, let's go. I don't want to stick around just to have coffee and cake with these people."

Ellen pulls her arm free from her husband's grip. "I want to stick around. You go ahead. Mary can take me home." Ellen knows that even the mention of her sister Mary's name raises the hair on the back of Billy's neck. The two of them never got along. For a moment, Ellen thinks Billy will grab her again and force her to leave with him.

"Whatever," Billy says. Ellen sees Billy's anger as he storms out of the Social Hall.

Ellen talks with a few community residents and then moves toward her sister, who has been sitting quietly in a chair along the wall. "You ready to go?"

"I've been ready for half an hour," Mary replies, "just been waiting for you. Do you want to stop for ice cream, or do we have to go to one of those health food snack restaurants you're always taking me to?"

"Ice cream's fine. You can order one of those triple scoop sundaes you like. I'll get a frozen yogurt."

"You may live longer than me," Mary says, "but I'll enjoy life more." Both women laugh.

* * *

The sisters sit at a table in Mimi's Ice Cream Shoppe. "Have you been able to talk with him yet about the money?" Mary asks.

"I've tried," Ellen responds, "but he always cuts me off. You know how he feels. For the past 20 years, you've made no secret of what you think of him. You believe he just sees me as a trophy wife."

"And do you see why?" Mary asks. "All he talks about are your good looks, usually in the crudest fashion. I heard what he said at the meeting. There are better ways to say that a woman is attractive then to call her hot in front of a room full of people."

"You're right, Sis, but that attitude isn't helping me get you the money you need."

"I guess I should try to be nicer to him. You know my problem. Warren died and left me with almost nothing. He depleted our savings and cashed out his life insurance to invest in that land deal that went bust. I don't know why I let him do it. I'm left with his debts and a house with a mortgage. $100,000 will allow me to get a fresh start. I know that Billy can afford it. My income from my waitressing job barely keeps me afloat. Can't you convince him to give me the money? Without it, I could lose everything."

Ellen places her hand over Mary's. "I'll try, Sweetie. I'll do my best, but he controls the money."

* * *

"All aboard," Professor Rita Diaz says, motioning for her Tuesday morning Botany class to board the bus for the field trip to the Perico Forest Preserve. Once the students are seated, she continues. "When we get to the preserve, you're to collect plant samples to take to the lab and analyze. You have already selected your teams. Each team has been assigned a plant classification. You'll collect plants, write a group report, and make a presentation to the class."

Rita turns to Donald Devries. "Many of you know Professor Devries from our Chemistry Department. A team from one of his classes has been assigned to work with you on the chemical makeup of your plants. Professor Trevor's students will help you with the computer applications you need to complete your analysis and prepare your presentations. A group from Mrs. Agnew's Dietetic Technician Certificate Program will be available to the team assigned to edible plants." Rita notices two of the boys from the edible plant team sit up and high five each other. She knows why these students are happy to hear that they will be working with Mrs. Agnew. "OK, boys, settle down. We'll be at the preserve in about 40 minutes."

When the bus reaches its destination, the door opens and the students and two professors stream out.

"You have two hours," Rita says, "and, remember, I'll be watching you."

"We know, Professor, from the sky," one of her students replies, glancing upward.

"Be very careful not to handle poisonous plants," Rita warns everyone as her students join their teams and move from the parking lot to the wooded area.

"Do you think we should go with them?" Donald asks as the students begin their search. "I remember, once, when I was on a college field trip, a group of us got lost. It took us three hours to find our way back, and one of my team, I won't say who, contracted a bad case of poison ivy."

"Field trips are different now, Don. Look up." Donald sees three small objects hovering over the section of the preserve where her students will be working. "You remember the other day, in the Faculty Lounge, Lionel said 'I'll be with you in cyberspace'. This is what he meant. Lionel arranged for Sherriff's Department drones to hover over our class and video them. One of Lionel's students, Adiva Fayed, is at the Sheriff's Department's Technology Center right now." Rita pulls her phone out of her hip pocket and pushes a few buttons. "You there, Adiva?"

"I'm here, professor. I'm sending the images to your phone."

"I see them."

Rita turns her attention back to Donald. "That's what I meant when I told the class I'd be watching them. If any of these students get lost, or in trouble, I'll know immediately. We've also implemented an additional precaution to ensure that no one touches poisonous plants. The Sheriff's Department has an application which identifies designated species. They use it to find illegal growth, such as marijuana. Lionel's students programmed it to send a signal to me and my class if one of them gets within ten feet of a poisonous plant. It also identifies the plant."

Rita and Donald return to the bus. Rita's phone buzzes three times, identifying poisonous plants, as they wait for the students to return. After slightly over two hours the students board the bus, their bags bulging, for the ride back to campus.

"I'll see you at the theater on Saturday," Donald says as he and Rita walk to their cars. "A matinee and evening performance and I'm still having problems with that long speech I have in the second act."

"You have four days and I'll work with you on it, Don. I'm sure you'll do just fine."

Emanuel

* * *

Park Ranger Jesse Valdez watches as visitors move toward the forest preserve's two exits. *There haven't been many visitors today*, he thinks. *There usually aren't on Fridays. School field trips come earlier in the week. Families arrive on weekends.* He will be making his final rounds in fifteen minutes. The ranger is responsible for ensuring that nobody remains after the preserve's closing, at 7:00. The preserve can be dangerous after dark. His job is to ensure everyone is safely on their way home.

Glancing in his rear-view mirror, he sees a car coming into the park rather than leaving. *This is strange*, he thinks. *Nobody enters the park this time of day. I'd better keep an eye on the car to make sure the visitor leaves before dark.*

Through his binoculars, Jesse sees the car's driver, wearing a hooded sweatshirt, emerge, take a trowel, lift something out of the ground, stuff it in a paper bag, and place the bag into the car's trunk. The driver re-enters the car, makes a U-turn, and heads for the exit. *It's probably nothing*, Jesse thinks, *but my orders are to note anything out of the ordinary.* He grabs the tablet from his car, taps a few keys, and enters the information about the last-minute visitor into the Park Service's database.

* * *

"And— curtain down," Stuart Abbott says as Billy's head drops to his chest. I pull the rope and the curtain falls on the Sun Coast Shores Community Theater's Saturday matinee. The actors hear the applause. "Curtain up," Stuart says. I pull the rope again. The cast bows. I pull the rope a third time to lower it.

"You guys did great!" Stuart high fives everyone in the cast.

"Lionel, you're the best curtain puller I've ever worked with," Rita says, tweaking my cheek as she passes.

"I guess I've found my calling."

18

The cast and crew gather backstage, preparing to pass the time before the evening performance. "Dinner's here," Ellen says as she opens the stage door for Mary, allowing her sister to bring the pizza boxes into the theater's lounge area, the aroma of cheese and mushrooms wafting through the room.

"There better be one with mushroom," Billy shouts. "Ellen, you know that I like lots of mushrooms on my pizza."

"I know, dear," Ellen replies, "we ordered one with mushrooms and one plain," then, turning toward her sister, "Tom having you do deliveries, now?"

"We're all doing double duty since CGI bought us, demanding lower costs and more profit, but I'm not complaining. It gets me out of the restaurant."

Rita picks up both boxes. "I'll put these in the microwave to re-heat them. That'll ensure they're piping hot."

"You're right," Ellen says. "Let me take one to the microwave in the men's dressing room. Rita, why don't you take the other to the microwave in the women's dressing room." Rita peaks into the top box and gives it to Ellen.

Stuart stands in front of the group, juts his chin upward, and grabs his jacket lapels. "When I toured with the American Shakespeare Company, Dame Regina Wentworth taught me the cardinal rule of the theater. 80% of acting is remembering your lines and not bumping into the furniture. You guys aced it on both counts."

The cast turns toward Stuart. They know what's coming. Rita and Ellen put their boxes down. Reheating will have to wait. For over ten minutes the director talks about his touring days. They've heard these stories before but, out of respect for their director, they always listen.

Emanuel

"Now let's relax and enjoy the pizza," Stuart says, after completing his dissertation.

Rita grabs the large tote bag she always carries, pulls out a pen and draws a diagonal line through the four vertical lines already on the paper. The cast has a pool, each cast member guessing how many times Stuart will mention his touring days. His comments a few minutes earlier were number fifteen. My guess is twenty-two, so I'm still in the running. I had googled Dame Regina Wentworth and discovered she was, in fact, a famous Shakespearian actress forty years ago and that Stuart had toured with her once, for about two months. The way their director tells the story, he and Dame Regina were bosom buddies who performed together for many years.

Rita and Ellen re-heat their pizzas, bring them out to the backstage area, and hand slices to the cast and crew.

"Did you ever notice," Rita turns to Ellen, as the two women sit with pizza on their laps, "it's always the women who serve the food as the men sit around waiting to be served."

"That's the way it is in our house," Ellen says. "If anything happened to me, I think Billy would just sit at the table waiting for dinner until he shriveled up and died." Both women laugh.

Billy pulls out a deck of cards. "Anyone for a friendly game of gin?" Stuart and two other cast members quickly accept. The four men sit at one of the bridge tables. Billy shuffles the cards and deals the first hand.

Billy puts the pizza slice in his mouth and is about to take a bite, then slams it back down on the plate. "It's cold," Billy shouts, pointing at Ellen. "Babe, take the damn thing and put it back in the microwave. You know I don't like it cold." Ellen grabs the paper plate from Billy's hand, storms into the women's dressing room, and returns two minutes later, shoving the plate in front of Billy, who attacks his slice, much like you might expect Henry VIII to attack a chicken leg.

20

The men have been playing cards for about fifteen minutes when Billy sits up, ramrod straight, an anguished look on his face.

"You feeling OK, Billy?" Stuart asks.

"I'm fine," Billy says, but the look on his face tells a different story. About three minutes later Billy stands in the middle of a hand and walks quickly toward the rest room. Stuart follows him. When the two men return, it's obvious Billy is not feeling well.

Ellen rushes over. "You OK, honey?"

"Yeah," Billy pushes his wife away.

"Billy, why don't you go lay down on the couch in my office?" Stuart says, pointing to a room just off the backstage area.

Billy walks slowly toward the room.

It's 6:15 and the cast is preparing for the evening performance. Billy emerges from Stuart's office. His face is ghost white.

"Are you going to be able to do the show?" Stuart asks. "You only have a few lines in the last act. I can go on for you."

"I'll be fine." The tone in Billy's voice is that of a man who has lived his life never ever admitting he's sick.

"That's the way Billy is," Ellen says to Rita. "He can never admit that he can't do something, even if it's a small part in a show I know he doesn't want to do."

The lights in the theater dim and the audience prepares for the evening performance. Billy sits backstage waiting for the final act. As the evening progresses Billy's skin becomes ashen. Stuart prepares to perform in his place but, when he hears his cue, Billy enters, haltingly, stage left.

"Dad," Laura places her arm on Billy's shoulder. "You can't keep drinking those beers. That's your third one this afternoon. You remember what the doctor said."

Emanuel

"Ah, what do them damn doctors know," Billy replies. "My father gave me my first beer when— when—,"

Watching from backstage, I see that Billy is not well. Laura will have to cover for him if he can't get through his lines.

"I know. Some of your best memories with grandpa were when you sat on the porch after dinner, drinking. But grandpa died of cirrhosis of the liver when he was only sixty-one. You're almost sixty. We'd like to have you around for a little longer."

"Don't worry, honey." Billy's voice is low and weak. "I'll be around for, for— a good, long—,"

I see the blank look in Billy's eyes. I'm sure Laura sees it, also. "And I know you want to see my son grow up, get married, and give you some great grandkids." Billy's head falls and he slumps in his chair as I lower the curtain.

The cast begins to assemble for their bows. I grab the rope which controls the curtain and am about to raise it.

"Stop!" Ellen shouts, as she rushes toward her husband, "Billy isn't moving."

Almost in unison, the cast turns toward the front of the stage where Billy sits motionless, his head lying on the table. Stuart places his index and middle fingers on Billy's throat, over the carotid artery. He grabs his phone and dials 911. "We need an ambulance at the Sun Coast Shores Community Theater, immediately." Stuart tries to keep his voice calm, but I can see his hands shake and sweat form on his brow. I instantly sense that Billy's condition is grave. Rita drapes her arm gently over Ellen's shoulder.

The paramedics arrive in less than fifteen minutes and immediately go to work on Billy. "I'm sorry ma'am," one of the paramedics says, kneeling on one knee in front of the sobbing Ellen. "There was nothing we could do. He died before we arrived."

One of the paramedics calls the Sheriff's Office. Twenty minutes later my friend, Sheriff Tony Maggio, and two deputies arrive.

"Has anyone left the theater?" Tony asks.

"Only the audience," Stuart replies. "Do you need to talk to them?"

"It would be helpful," Tony says.

"Most of them paid by credit card so we can find them if we need them," Stuart responds.

Tony and his deputy speak to each member of the cast to learn what happened and take their statements.

"I took some photos and videos back stage after the show," Laura says, handing Tony her phone. "Will this help?"

"Yes," Tony responds," taking her phone. "Lionel, can you help me send these pictures to our department web site. I'm still learning how to do this stuff."

"Sure."

Four other cast members and the stage manager also used their phone's camera to record backstage activities. I help Tony upload this material to the Sheriff's Department's server.

"How did he die?" Stuart asks.

"We'll know better after the Medical Examiner completes her work up," Tony answers.

It's just after 11:00 PM when Tony and his deputies complete their initial investigation and tell everyone to go home. Rita ensures that Ellen will stay with her sister for a while.

Tony and I walk to our cars together. "We still on for dinner on Saturday, Lionel?" Tony asks.

"We are. Maybe you'll have some information from your Medical Examiner by then."

* * *

"When the moon hits your eye—," Tony sings as he and I sit in his family room, waiting for dinner. The thick, shag carpet and leather sofa and love seat give a warm, homey feeling to the room. The beautiful art work, much of it painted by his wife, Marie, add a touch of elegance.

"—like a big pizza pie," I chime in. "You still got it, my friend, just like when we sang in the University chorus."

My wife, Deb, who has been helping Marie in the kitchen, pokes her head out. "I seem to remember that the chorus director placed both of you Carusos in the back row and told you to sing low. I believe his exact words were 'you both have pleasant voices— but don't give up your day jobs.'"

Tony and I look at each other and smile. As usual, Deb is right.

"You look the same as you did thirty years ago when you were teaching criminology at Franklin University and I was a member of the University Police force," Tony says.

"Well, my hair's a little grayer, actually, a lot grayer," I say.

"But other than that, you look the same. I, on the other hand, never went gray," Tony rubs his bald head, "and I've gained a few pounds, thanks to Marie's pasta."

"I'm glad we stayed in touch, Tony. I've used many of the stories you told me about your work here with the Sheriff's Department in my classes, and, when you were elected Sheriff, Deb and I figured this must be a safe place to retire."

"And I'm glad you chose to join us on Florida's west coast, but doesn't retirement mean you don't work? You spent your career as a college professor, and now you're teaching at Tampa Bay Community College. How did that happen?"

"I missed teaching, so I went to talk to the folks at the college. They were looking for someone to create and teach a Forensic Technology Workshop and the rest, as they say, is history. Most of the kids in the workshop come from lower income families and must work to pay for school and help support their families. They know that college is their ticket to a good life, and they're determined to succeed."

As usual, the dinner Deb and Marie prepares is delicious. Tony and I are in the kitchen, cleaning up, when Tony's phone buzzes, signaling a text message from his office. He pulls the phone from his pocket, taps a few keys, and scrolls.

"I believe we have a *Tech Squad* workshop this week," he says.

"We do."

"Then we have a case for your students."

"We're ready."

* * *

As Tony and I enter the Sheriff's Department's Technology Center one of my students, Diego Rivera, is holding court, as he often does before the workshop begins. I've developed personal nicknames for many of my students. Diego's nickname is *leader of the pack*. Whatever the situation, Diego takes command.

"*Ven y lomalo*," Diego says, waving his hand over the folding table sitting against the Technology Center's back wall. Diego stands silent for a few seconds, enjoying the puzzled look on the other's faces. "That's 'come and get it' in Spanish for all of you illiterates who only speak one language."

"I speak four languages." Adiva Fayad gently pokes Diego's ribs. "I guess that makes you the *ba swad*. That's illiterate in Farsi."

"We've got pulparino tamarind candies, chiki chocolate cookies, Mexican snack chips, and my grandma's homemade salsa."

I'm enjoying the banter among the students who make up *The Tech Squad*. When I organized the workshop, the students began bringing snacks. The group's diversity means that the food each student has eaten from birth is often unknown to the others. The small talk around the

25

snack table creates a bond among these young people, which helps them work together as a team.

"Are your snacks going to burn my mouth?" Judy Levinson asks.

"Of course not," Diego replies. "My grandma would never want to hurt any of my friends." He then turns toward the others with a broad grin on his face. "Of course, Aunt Isabella helps grandma with the salsa, and she doesn't always approve of my friends."

Alex Perez turns toward me. "Do we have a case today, Doc?"

"We do."

James rubs is hands. "I hope it's a murder."

"It is."

Each student sits at a computer terminal linked to projection equipment which displays images on one or more of the eight screens positioned on the Technology Center's four walls. Tony got the *Tech Squad* authorization to view evidence he and his deputies see.

"Sheriff, what do you have for us?" I ask.

"I'm sure you've all read in the local newspaper about the murder at the Sun Coast Shores Community Theater," Tony answers.

A big smile crosses Diego's face. "Newspaper, what's a newspaper?"

Judy plays along with Diego's joke. "Come on, D, you were in history class when we talked about it. It's the way people used to find out what's happening in the world, before the Internet. My grandpa sits in a chair every day and folds and refolds this newspaper thing. I showed him how he could get the same information from my phone."

"Did he get a phone?" Diego asks.

"No, he still reads that newspaper."

"Anyway," Tony continues, "after Billy Agnew died, my deputies and I secured the crime scene and interviewed the play's cast and crew. We confiscated the food in the backstage area since it's possible he died from something

Murder At The Playhouse

he ate. We also downloaded pictures and videos the cast and crew took back stage. Our Medical Examiner has since determined that Billy died from poison mushrooms which, we suspect, he ingested when eating pizza after a performance at the theater."

"Did anyone else eat the pizza?" James asks.

"Everyone had at least one slice."

"So, why didn't anyone else get sick or die?" Alex inquires.

"We don't know."

"What have you discovered so far?" Diego questions.

"We know that the pizza came from Giovani's. A restaurant employee, Mary, delivered it. Two of the cast members, Rita Diaz and Ellen Agnew, Billy's wife, placed slices on paper plates and served it to everyone."

"Is that Professor Diaz, the Botany Professor?" Adiva asks. "I helped her with a field trip."

"It is," Tony responds.

"Is she a suspect?"

"I guess she is. Anyway, we assume that, either poison mushrooms were on the pizza before it arrived, or someone put them on one of Billy's slices at the theater. Once we learned that Billy was murdered, we got subpoenas for the financial records of the cast and crew and Giovanni employees who handled the pizzas. Billy's net worth is slightly over $1.5 million, so money could be the motive. We also got warrants for their, what's it called, professor?"

"I think the term you're looking for is social media presence."

"Yeah," Tony says, glancing toward his deputies and pointing at me, "what he said. That's where the investigation stands."

"OK, Tech Squad," I say, "this is where you come in. How can we help solve this murder?"

Emanuel

"On the cop shows I watch, the spouse is always the first suspect," Judy says, picking her head up from focusing on her phone. My nickname for Judy is *The Fiddler,* because her head is always pointed down during these workshops so she could fiddle with her phone and, yet, she's an excellent student. I'm amazed how students like Judy can simultaneously focus on their phones and pay attention to what's being said. "Let's see what we can learn about Mrs. Agnew from her online presence." Judy plugs her phone into her computer and presses a few keys. Ellen's social media accounts, such as Facebook and Twitter, display for all to see.

"Wow!" I can see James' eyes widen as he leans toward the computer screen.

"Wow is right," Diego and Alex chime in, almost in unison. "She's hot."

Judy places her hands on her hips. "Would you guys get your minds out of the gutter and see what you can find that might help the case?"

"She's much younger than him," James says. "You might call her a trophy wife. Her emails and text messages to her sister indicate he usually ignores her except when he wants—,"

"We get the point!" Judy snaps.

"I might be able to shed some light on their relationship," I say. I log onto the Sun Coast Shores Community Facebook page and find the video of the recent meeting when Ellen spoke.

"He really insulted her," Judy observes, "and there's something else pointing to the wife. She's a nutritionist. She would know about poison mushrooms."

"There's more," Tony continues. "Mrs. Agnew will inherit his entire estate and collect on his $250,000 life insurance policy and, once we determined he was poisoned, she sued Giovani's. She's asking for $5 million."

"Maybe pictures from the confiscated phones will tell us something," Alex says. "I bet even old people, eh—," Alex looks at Tony, his deputies, and me, "—adults use their phones to take pictures. Can anyone see where Mrs. Agnew had the opportunity to put mushrooms on Mr. Agnew's pizza?"

"I think I can help with that," Tony offers. "One of the new gizmos we have allows us to load multiple photos and videos and synchronize them. We can view a scene from multiple angles and perspectives."

"Great," I say. "Let's boot it up and see the pictures and videos from everyone's camera."

"Unfortunately," Tony replies, "nobody here has figured out how to use it."

James raises his hand as he sits up straight in this chair. "I can help."

I'm not surprised that James is familiar with this new type of photographic technology. My nickname for James is *first adapter*. If new technology comes on the market, James jumps on it. It takes him about fifteen minutes to load pictures and videos that had been downloaded from the cast and crew's phones into the application, called Photomesh, which produces a 3D video which displays on the Technology Center's eight screens.

"That's cool," Diego says. "This application, what's it called, James?"

"Photomesh."

"This Photomesh puts us right in the middle of the crime scene," Diego continues, as he swings his chair around to view all eight screens. Although some pictures display that aren't related to the murder scene, most show the backstage area just prior to Billy's death.

"The video shows an eleven-minute period from the time the pizza was delivered until everyone was ready to eat," James says. "They appear to be listening to some old guy talking about touring with someone named Dame

29

Regina, whoever that is. Mrs. Agnew and Professor Diaz then took the pizzas to microwave ovens to warm them up. Mrs. Agnew could have put the mushrooms on Billy's slice when she took it out of the oven."

"Can we see who gave Mr. Agnew his pizza?" Alex asks.

"Professor Diaz handed Billy his plate," James notes, "but he gave it to his wife to re-heat. You can see from the video she was pissed at the way he was treating her."

"Let's try this," I say. "How about if each of you see what's out there in cyberspace on the other cast members and crew. Is there anyone else with a motive?"

"You were in the cast and were part of the crew, professor," Diego observes. "Should we be looking at you?"

"You should."

The students turn their attention to their computers, their fingers moving quickly over their keyboards.

"I've got something," Alex says. "Mary, the Giovanni's employee who delivered the pizza, is Mrs. Hot—," Alex glances at me, "—Mrs. Agnew's sister. Her financial records show she is deeply in debt. She's maxed out her credit cards and she's two months behind with her mortgage payments. Emails and texts between her and her sister show she has asked Mrs. Agnew for help. Mrs. Agnew wants to help, but Billy refuses. Billy's death appears to solve her problem."

Diego is the next student with an observation. "I got some information about Giovanni's. The restaurant's supplier has six claims against it for delivering food that did not meet Health Department standards in the last three months. They appear to have lax quality control, so it's possible the restaurant received poison mushrooms."

"We thought about that," Tony says, "but, then, why would only Mr. Agnew's slice be contaminated. If the restaurant or its supplier were responsible, more than one person would have become ill and, possibly, died."

"I may have something," James offers. "Professor Devries, who teaches Chemistry at our school, was in the cast. I googled his name and found a police report accusing Mr. Agnew of harassing his daughter."

"I remember that," Tony replies. "Unfortunately, we couldn't do anything. The professor was mad as hell at Billy but what Billy did wasn't against the law."

"And Professor Trevor's video of the Community Meeting shows that Mr. Agnew made crude remarks about his daughter," Judy adds.

"That does give Professor Devries a motive," Tony says. "Let's keep him on the suspect list."

"As you can see," Tony continues, "Mrs. Agnew, Professor Devries, and Mary all had motives. Since only Mrs. Agnew and Professor Diaz could have put the mushroom on Billy's pizza, we're back to Mrs. Agnew as the prime suspect."

Adiva Fayad had not spoken during this discussion. She listened and took in everything the other students said. She suddenly bolts up in her chair and stares at one of the screens containing Photomesh images. I'd seen this before. My nickname for Adiva is *The Quiet One*. She often sits silently during our workshops and absorbs what Tony, his deputies, and her fellow students say. She then suggests something that shows a completely new way of attacking a problem.

"So far," Adiva says, "we've been focusing on motive. Let's look at this from another angle, the murder weapon. Specifically, where did the murderer get the mushrooms? I think I may know. Sheriff, can you get warrants for the GPS tracking systems on each of our suspect's cars?"

"I can," Tony answers.

* * *

It's 5:00 on a Tuesday afternoon. Professor Diaz is cleaning the botany lab after her last class and anxious to go home. She will be preparing dinner for Donald

31

Emanuel

Devries. She hopes that the shy Chemistry professor will take the hint and spend the night.

"Professor Rita Diaz?"

Rita looks up from her plants. She recognizes the two men entering her classroom as Sheriff Maggio and one of his deputies.

"Yes."

"You're under arrest."

The professor feels the blood pounding through her body. "For what?"

"Murder," the sheriff replies.

* * *

The *Tech Squad*, along with Tony and his deputies, are assembled for our weekly workshop.

"OK, students, let's get to work," I say. "Last week Adiva asked the sheriff to get warrants for our suspect's GPS systems. Four days ago, the sheriff arrested Professor Diaz for the murder. Adiva, please explain to the rest of the workshop why you asked the sheriff to get the warrants and how you broke the case open."

"We focused on Mrs. Agnew," Adiva says, "because she's the only suspect with motive who could have placed the mushrooms on Billy's pizza. But how did she get them? I decided to try to find out where they came from."

"I remembered that the drone videos I took during Professor Diaz's class field trip showed poison mushrooms at Perico Forrest Preserve. I assumed that it was possible that this was the source. I asked the sheriff to allow me to re-photograph the area of the preserve where they grew." Adiva displays the videos showing the section of the preserve containing the poison mushrooms during the field trip and the same section last week. "As you can see, they were there during the field trip. The second video shows dirt where they used to be."

Adiva then displays a GPS application. "I knew that Professor Devries helped Professor Diaz during her class's field trip. Therefore, both Professor Diaz and

Professor Devries knew their location. I looked at the GPS system records from both of their cars. Since Mrs. Agnew was also a suspect, I looked at her GPS data, as well. Professor Diaz returned to the preserve at 6:30 on the Friday after her field trip, arriving just before closing."

"When Adiva told me what she found," Tony says, "I asked the Park Ranger Service if they had any information about someone entering the preserve late that day. It appears that the Park Ranger on duty had posted an entry on their web site saying someone had entered the park at the time that Professor Diaz's GPS says she was there."

Adiva continues. "Professor Devries didn't return to the preserve and Mrs. Agnew was never there."

"Can we prove that she took the mushrooms from the preserve?" Judy asks.

"When we arrested Professor Diaz," Tony says, "we got a warrant to search her car. There were trace amounts of the mushrooms in the trunk."

"And how did she get them into the theater?" Diego asks.

Adiva displays the video the Photomesh software had created. "Look at the tote bag Professor Diaz uses. She brought them into the theater in that bag. The sheriff's warrants allowed him to search Professor Diaz's tote bag. The evidence was right there."

Adiva continues her explanation. "As soon as Mary delivered the pizza, the professor immediately took both boxes and suggested they be put in the microwave oven." Adiva pauses the Photomesh video. "Here, we see her lifting the top of the box. She wants to be sure she will re-heat the mushroom pizza. She gave the other box to Mrs. Agnew. Her plan was to add the mushrooms to a slice she would give to Billy." Adiva continues running the video. "We see her giving Billy his plate. Although there is no video of Professor Diaz reheating the pizza, we can assume she added them to the slice she would give to Billy."

"Wouldn't that cast suspicion on her?" James asks.

"I think I can answer that," I reply. "My pizza was hot. When Adiva told me what she had found, I checked with the other members of the cast and crew. Only Billy's was cold. We suspect she removed one slice before putting it into the microwave, knowing that Billy would want it re-heated. She also assumed that he would tell Ellen to re-heat it. She was right on both counts."

"How did Professor Diaz know that Billy would want mushrooms on his pizza and that he would return it if it isn't hot?" Judy asks. "It wouldn't do her any good to bring the mushrooms if Billy didn't like them, or if he didn't demand that it be re-heated."

I continue. "Ellen suggested that she and Billy go out for pizza after one of our rehearsals. She made a point that Billy likes mushrooms and that he demands it be hot. She commented that Billy returns it if it isn't. I'm sure the professor heard her say that."

"But what about motive?" Alex asks. "We still don't have a motive."

* * *

November 1982 Florida West Coast University,

He bends his knees and balances on his toes, the knuckles of his clenched fist extending outward from his torso, just like coach had taught him. He could see the glare in the eyes and smell the sweat of the cornerback standing approximately three feet in front of him. Four seconds to go, down by four, and no timeouts left. Coach had ordered the torpedo forty-nine left play where the quarterback fakes a handoff and then fires a pass to the wide receiver. He's ready. Either he would score and make them champs, or their season would end just like last year, second in the conference.

"Huh!" he hears the quarterback shout. As the ball is snapped, he takes a step forward, then veers left. The

Murder At The Playhouse
defender hesitates for a split second, just enough time for
him to barrel forward and race down field. *This is it,* he
thinks. He hugs the sideline and counts, one-one
thousand, two-one thousand, three-one thousand, four-
one thousand, and turns, just like coach had taught him.
His heart sinks. The ball is about ten feet in front of him,
but almost a foot over his head. He bends his leg, raises
his left arm, and jumps, just like coach had taught him.
He curls his fingers. The ball touches his fingertips. He
thinks he failed, the ball would roll off his fingers and fall
to the turf, an incomplete pass, game over, but,
miraculously, the ball doesn't fall. He holds the ball and
cradles it to his body. It's almost impossible to catch a
football with one hand, but he just did. Wow! He turns
toward the goal post. He sees a linebacker, a mountain of
a man, about ten feet up field and headed right for him.
He has no place to go, no way to avoid being pushed out-
of-bounds. It would be game over. He hopes he'll come
out of it with all his body parts intact. He sees his
opponent square his shoulders and prepare to lunge
forward. He braces for the impact, but the impact never
comes. He watches, in what seems like slow motion, and
sees the linebacker's left foot get caught in front of his
right. The big man goes down. He leaps over the fallen
hulk. Coach had never taught him this move, it's all his.
There's nothing between him and victory but grass. As he
crosses the goal line, he can hear his teammates, and
over five-thousand fans, scream. They're champs. And
now there would be a victory party. He'll take full
advantage of his new-found role as hero.

The party is in full swing when he enters the fraternity
house. He isn't two feet inside when one of the
cheerleaders approaches, rubbing against him as she
hands him a beer. *This is going to be a hell of a victory
party*, he thinks.

35

Emanuel

"All hail the conquering hero," one of his teammates shouts, raising a beer mug. He doesn't know the kid's name, one of the bench warmers, not a real gladiator, like him. He doesn't know how much time has passed. He holds his third, or is it his fourth, beer in one hand, the hand that had pulled down the pass, and a joint in another, his second. Two cheerleaders are hanging all over him. It's time. He leads one of them upstairs. She doesn't resist. He pushes her to the bed, jumps on top of her and grabs to yank her panties down, only to discover she isn't wearing any. He pulls his own pants down. Pinning her shoulders to the mattress, he's ready. Then nothing. He tries everything. He can't perform. After what seems like an eternity, he stops, disgusted with himself. She pushes him off and storms out of the room.

The bitch better not say anything, he thought.

He stays at the party for another hour, everyone talking about the game, but he hardly hears a word. He even refuses more beer and joints. There's one big perk to scoring a final touchdown and he blew it.

He leaves the party alone. As he walks back to the dorm, he feels life returning to his groin, with a vengeance. *Shit*, he thinks, *it's too late, but maybe not*. As he passes the library, he sees her. It's dark and she's alone. There's no one else around. He grabs her from behind and pushes her down. They're between the library wall and three large bushes. He grabs her shoulders. A necklace she'd wearing breaks and falls to the ground. It's over in less than two minutes. He gets up and walks away, taking the necklace as a souvenir. *Tonight wasn't a total loss, after all*, he thinks.

* * *

The ringing of the phone wakes the little girl. She looks to the empty bed next to her, her sister's bed. She can't wait until she's big like her sister and can stay out late. She wants to be just like her when she grows up. She's still groggy when mama opens the door to her room.

36

"Get dressed pollita," momma says. "We're going for a car ride."

She knows something's wrong. Even an eight-year-old can sense the stress in mama's voice. Mama and papa place her in the car's back seat. No one speaks as they drive. Mama always talks when they're in the car, but not tonight. Papa parks the car and they enter a big building. She's frightened. What is this? What's wrong?

"Stay here, pollita," mama sits her down in a big chair. She sees mama and papa go into a room. She can see through the room's windows that they were talking with a man and a woman in white coats and a man in a uniform holding a pad and a pencil. Her big sister is sitting on the bed? *Why is her sister in this bed? Why isn't she home in her own bed.* She jumps off the chair and runs into the room, grabbing mama as tight as she can. She looks at her sister. What's wrong? The little girl grabs the pendant around her neck. Mama calls it a nervous habit.

At almost the same time, her sister grabs at her throat. "It's gone," the older girl screams. "He took it!"

* * *

Current Day

"Finding the motive," Tony replies, in response to Alex's question, "is where good old-fashioned police work comes in. After Adiva pointed out that Professor Diaz is the only suspect who appears to have access to poison mushrooms and could have put them on Mr. Agnew's pizza, we looked into the professor's background. Adiva, I'll tell the story, but I need you to help me at the computer. I'm still all thumbs when dealing with the keyboard and, what do you call that other thing."

"A mouse, sir."

"Yeah, a mouse. Anyway, at first, the professor's background showed no connection between her and Mr. Agnew, other than the play. We then dug deeper and

found our motive. Adiva, please display the police report."
Adiva displays an electronic copy of a faded document.
"The professor's name is associated with an old case, a
rape case over forty years ago, of one Hope Diaz, at
Florida West Coast University. Adiva, please scroll to the
next page. This shows the notes the detective took on the
case. The professor was a child at the time, and she
accompanied her mother and father to the hospital after
her sister was raped. Hope told the detective that the
rapist had taken her necklace."

"Was the case ever solved?" Judy asks.

"No, it wasn't," Tony replies. "That's why we have it on
the computer. When we, what do you call it, professor?"

"Digitized," I say.

"Yeah, digitized. When we digitized the department
files, we copied all cold cases into the computer."

Adiva continues. "I helped Professor Diaz when her
mother died. Her mother had been asking for Hope. The
professor said that Hope was her sister, who had died."

"So, what does that have to do with Mr. Agnew?" Judy
asks. "I'm still not seeing a motive."

"School records show that Hope Diaz and Mr. Agnew
attended Florida West Coast University at the same time.
Those old police records also show that Hope Diaz
committed suicide five years after the rape. Her father
hounded the sheriff's office for almost twenty years,
asking about the rape case. Notes in the detective's file
show that the family believed that Hope's rape caused her
to commit suicide. 'If the bastard is ever caught,' her
father had said, 'we want him charged with murder.'"

"But why did Professor Diaz believe that Mr. Agnew
raped her sister?" James asks.

Adiva displays an enlarged selfie that Ellen had taken
of herself and Professor Diaz.

"When we were watching the video from the Photomesh
software," Adiva continues, "I saw a photo that Mrs.
Agnew took with Professor Diaz. Mrs. Agnew sent the

professor a copy of that picture. I noticed the initials on their necklace pendants. They look alike, except for the letters. Professor Diaz is wearing an M, Mrs. Agnew is wearing an E. I showed this picture to the sheriff."

Tony picks up the story. "I took the picture to a jeweler who said that these two pieces appeared to be handmade, probably by the same person. When I questioned Professor Devries, he said that Professor Diaz told him that her mother made jewelry, which she and her sister wore. When Professor Diaz saw the pendant Mrs. Agnew was wearing, she knew that it was her sister's and that Mr. Agnew must have taken it when he raped her. There's the motive."

"I'm confused," Judy says. "The professor's sister's name was Hope. Mrs. Agnew's name is Ellen and she wore an E pendant."

"D," Adiva gestures toward Diego, "Can you answer Judy's question about the initials?"

"I can," Diego replies. "You can see from the photo that professor Diaz is wearing an M pendant even though her name is Rita." Diego presses a few keys on his keyboard. A school faculty list displays. "Professor Diaz is listed as Margarita 'Rita' Diaz. Rita is an anglicized version of Margarita. When Professor Diaz saw Mrs. Agnew's pendant, she knew that it had belonged to her sister."

"How?" Judy asks.

"The professor's mother made the jewelry using the letters of their given names, not their anglicized names," Diego answers. "Hope was wearing the E pendant when she was raped because Hope is the English translation of her given name, Esperanza."

I stand in the center of the Technology lab. "You guys should be proud of yourselves. You just used your knowledge of technology to help the Sheriff's Department solve a murder. How 'bout we celebrate. I'll order out for pizza."

Emanuel

"Hold the mushrooms," Diego says, to the delight of everyone in the room.

MURDER BY THE LAKE

The Tech Squad has mixed feelings about their role in the murder case at our local playhouse. They feel good about using technology to help solve the crime, but they hate having implicated Professor Diaz. I point out to them that criminals are not all drug dealers and low lives. If they're to become criminal investigators, they'll be dealing with all types of people. Simply put, if someone commits a crime, that person should go to jail.

The young men in the workshop were overjoyed that Mrs. Agnew will still be teaching in the Nutritionist Technician Certificate Program. They even asked if they can take one of her classes as an elective.

The next case proves even more stressful for the students because it hits much closer to home.

* * *

"Welcome to the Military Veteran's Club." Greg Ziegler reaches for the outstretched hand of Dave Shuster, the club's president. "I don't think I've seen you before." Dave glances at Greg's name tag. "Is this your first meeting, Greg?"

"It is."

"How long have you lived here."

"I closed on my home two weeks ago, February 27, to be exact. My realtor gave me a list of community activities. I figure joining some clubs is a good way to meet people."

"Your realtor's absolutely correct. Our veteran's group meets here in the Clubhouse's All-purpose room on the second Wednesday of every month. Where did you serve?"

Greg feels that familiar knot in his stomach. "Vietnam, '67 to '69."

Emanuel

"You'll find many of our club's members share your experience. You married, have kids, grandkids? We have a joint outing with the Fishing Club around Christmas when our families are here. The kids fish and us old guys share war stories. Sometimes the kids listen to these stories. My grandson, Ralph, has used what he's heard on these trips in term papers for his history class. I haven't the heart to tell him that many of the tales we tell may be less than 100% factual. However, he gets *A's* in history, so I guess his teachers believe grandpas never lie to their grandkids." Both men laugh, recognizing that the mind often enhances long-ago exploits as the years pass.

Greg hesitates for a moment. He is used to the questions about family, but it never gets any easier. "Nope, a confirmed bachelor." This is the line Greg always uses when asked about family. He doesn't like to think about what really happened.

At age 72, Greg fits right in with other Sun Coast retirees. The hair he still has is greying, and the size thirty-four waist slacks are consigned to Goodwill, replaced by size thirty-eight.

"Smile," Sandra Paulson says. Greg and Dave turn to see a woman holding a video camera. "This is for posterity." Greg hears the soft purring of the camera for approximately ten seconds, after which Sandra walks away.

"Sandra's the president of the Photography Club," Dave says. "She's taking still pictures and videos to post on the community web site. Well, come on in and mingle. Tonight's speaker is a recently retired army officer. He'll be talking about the newest ordnance the Defense Department uses in the fight against ISIS."

Greg walks to the refreshment table, pours a cup of coffee into a paper cup and reaches for a piece of cake.

A tall, slender man in khaki slacks and a Tampa Bay Rays tee shirt moves beside him. "My wife made that cake."

42

Greg turns toward the man, his eyes widen. He drops the cake and full coffee cup, spilling its hot liquid contents on the floor. He spins on his heels, completing a perfect military about face, and storms out of the room.

Greg can't sleep that night. He can feel his blood pressure rise, his mind returning to that day, over fifty years ago, in that Asian jungle, when he felt his world crumble. As the sun enters his bedroom window the next morning, he knows what he must do. It will be risky and take research and planning, but he has no choice. Fate has led him to this place at this time. Just before 11:00 he falls into a deep sleep, not waking until it's time to prepare dinner.

* * *

June 1968 – Dong Nai Province, Vietnam

I'm scared. I can't admit it to anyone. A soldier is trained to never show fear. That's what my father, who lost three toes to frostbite at Korea's Chosin reservoir, told me. That's what the sergeant in basic training told me. But now, here I am, sweating like a pig, crouched down, cradling my M16 rifle, and weighed down by six M67 grenades hanging from my cartridge belt. I'm waiting to board the helos that are to take my squad and me into the damp, bug infested Vietnamese jungle on yet another search and destroy mission.

My dad had been proud when I told him I wanted to join the Army after I graduated high school. "I might even want a military career," I told him.

My mother was not happy. She wanted me to go to college. In high school, I had been president of the Technology Club. She thought that should be my career. Dad and I told her that the Army would teach me to use computers and pay for college when I got out. That convinced her, sort of. After basic training I was sent for advanced instruction in computer technology. But, after completing training, with the Asian war raging, I was transferred to an Infantry unit, promoted to sergeant, and sent to this God forsaken hell hole.

I signal my squad to move forward. We duck-walk, bending low to avoid the copter's swirling blades, the wind almost blowing me over.

As we secure ourselves, preparing to lunge upward, we hear the Huey gunships pounding what will be our landing zone.

The helos fly at tree top-level. It takes less than fifteen minutes to reach the line of departure, the imaginary line when our unit can't turn back. I signal my squad to lock and load. We reach the landing zone. The chopper blades flatten the elephant grass as we exit the helo and prepare to move toward the village of Bien Hoa. The copters fly back to the base. Even with my squad, and the rest of C Company, scrambling to form up, I feel alone.

Our mission is to surround the village of Quan Tre and kill VC fighters and sympathizers. We never know what to look for. The enemy wears no uniform. They look like regular villagers, some as young as ten years old. The locals feed them, protect them, and give them shelter. They hide weapons in the foliage, so we can't see them, then whip them out and fire.

"What are we supposed to do, kill anyone we see?" I had asked the lieutenant back at the base.

"Every last one of them," he had answered.

"Even children?"

"They're all VC, you asshole. Kill them all. We need the body count."

The Lieutenant's a prick who will put his men in harm's way, so he can show the brass confirmed kills.

"Move out," the Lieutenant shouts.

We advance no more than one hundred yards when the ambush begins. The gunfire seems to come from everywhere and nowhere. I hit the ground, mud splattering over my uniform and face. I hear gun fire and see the flash from the VC's rifles, but I can't see them. They're spraying

44

us with automatic weapons fire and then fading back into the jungle.

A bouncing betty detonates. These mines jump from the ground two or three feet when triggered and rip a man's gut open when they explode. I turn toward an anguished scream. I see Private Fiorino, at least I think it's the private. His face is covered in blood. His leg is severed and there's a large hole in his stomach, gushing blood as if from a hose. I rush toward him. I go less than ten feet when I feel a sharp, white-hot pain in my right side.

* * *

Current Day

As I enter the Sun Coast Shores Social Hall for the Community Association meeting, I spot Greg Ziegler, one of our newer residents and the most recent member of the college faculty. "Over here, Greg," I say, signaling him to sit next to me. "Again, thanks for agreeing to make a presentation to my Tech Squad workshop. I really appreciate it."

"Glad I can help, Lionel."

"OK, calm down everyone," Morris Greenberg, the Community Association President, says, adjusting the podium microphone. "We have one item on the agenda this evening, the July 4th celebration. It may seem a little early to be talking about July 4th during the second week in April, but we have a lot of work to do." He points at Sandra Paulson. "Sandra will be recording everything we say and do for the community web site so, guys, be on your best behavior."

"Do we girls have to be on our best behavior, too?" a voice from the back of the room asks.

"We know you ladies are always on your best behavior, Jill," Morris replies, "it's the guys I worry about. Moving on, Jim Gilliam is chairman of the July 4th Planning Committee." Morris motions for Jim to join him at the podium.

45

Emanuel

"Thanks, Morris. Our celebration will begin with our annual brunch at 10:30 in the morning."

"What's on the menu?" a voice from the back of the room asks.

"The usual," Jim responds. "Eggs, bacon, sausage, pancakes, french toast, and oatmeal with lots of butter and cream, everything our doctors and wives tell us we shouldn't eat. I suggest you all take an extra cholesterol pill before you come." Jim hears a few snickers from the audience.

"We're going to need volunteers to prepare and serve the meal. Adele Becker has agreed to organize the helpers. Adele, please stand up." A tall, slender woman rises from her chair and nods.

"Same pay as last year, Jim?" a voice from the front row asks.

"Yup, same as last year, our undying gratitude. After brunch, we'll go to the pool and athletic area for our annual Senior Games Tournament. So, get your bocce ball, water volleyball, pickle ball, tennis, and shuffleboard teams together. My wife, Claudine, will be serving as Sports Commissioner for these events. And, Andy," Jim continues, pointing at a bald, somewhat overweight, resident toward the back of the room, "please don't wear your Speedo bathing suit again this year in the water volleyball match. It's really not a pretty sight." The meeting attendees erupt in laughter, the loudest coming from Andy.

"The games should be over by about 3:00. We'll reassemble on the Great Lawn at 8:00 to watch the Boston Pops Fourth of July concert on the big screen we've rented. I want to thank Lionel Trevor and his students," he says, gesturing toward me, "for volunteering to work with our local cable company to set up the screen, and Jesse Albertson for arranging our community fireworks, which will display during the concert. And Dennis," Jim gestures toward Dennis

46

MacBride, "with your new interest in photography, will you be working with Sandra to get shots of the fireworks?"

"I'm going to have to decline the offer," Dennis answers. "I plan to sit on my bench by the big lake, watch the display, and fish."

"Don't worry, Morris," Sandra says, peeking from behind her camera, "We should be able to get enough volunteers. Dennis, enjoy your fishing."

"What's happening between 3:00 and 8:00?" Andy, the man who wore the Speedo bathing suit, asks.

"We'll all be going home and taking our naps," Jim responds.

After the laughter dies down, Dave Shuster raises his hand. "Morris, what are we doing about the celebratory gun fire, you know our neighbors shooting their guns in the air? It seems to happen every year."

The gathering's lighthearted atmosphere immediately turns serious. Sun Coast Shores is a community built near fruit and vegetable farms. Many of the farm workers celebrate by firing guns into the air. Two years earlier a Sun Coast Shores maintenance worker found a bullet on the lawn of one of the homes near the edge of the community. Last year a young boy in a neighboring town was seriously injured by gun fire.

"That's the next item I want to discuss. I've invited Sheriff Tony Maggio to talk to us about this problem."

Tony approaches the speaker's lectern. "We've talked to the farm owners and the union leaders and explained that firing guns in the air is illegal. We've scheduled deputies to patrol the evening and night of the fourth. We will arrest anyone we see breaking that law."

"What if you don't see them?" Dave asks. "If you have a bullet, can't you identify the gun that shot the bullet? I know the cops do that on TV."

47

Emanuel

"If we have an intact bullet and a gun, we can match the bullet to the gun. Even if we only have a bullet fragment, we can often determine the type of firearm used. Unfortunately, in the case of the boy who was injured, and the bullet found on your property last year, we had no way of identifying the gun."

"Can't you look for guns registered to people who live in the farming community and examine them to find the one that shot the bullet?" one of the residents asks.

"I wish we could," Tony answers, "but there's a little thing called the Second Amendment to the Constitution. We can't just demand to see people's guns. We need probable cause."

"So, how do you keep those guys from shooting, and possibly hurting, or even killing, someone?" a voice from the fifth row asks.

"We'll do everything we can," Tony answers, "but we can't guarantee that they'll be no incidents."

A booming voice comes from the back of the room. "We'll take care of it ourselves." Everyone knows who's speaking even before they turn toward Steve Dombrowski. "You do what you can, sheriff. We'll take care of the rest."

* * *

"I see you've already met our newest Tech Squad member, Kayla Morgan," I say, as Tony and I enter the Sheriff's Department's Technology Center. The five members of the Tech Squad, six now that Kayla has joined, along with Tony's deputies, are gathered around the snack table.

At 6'2", Kayla towers above the other Tech Squad members. My personal nickname for Kayla is *The Jock*. She's the starting forward on the college's women's basketball team and led them to the state championship last year.

"These are delicious," Judy Levinson says, gesturing to Kayla, who brought the snacks. "Did you make them?"

Kayla smiles. "I did, but my mom and grandma hovered over me the whole time. They often tell me I do many things very well, but cooking isn't one of them. So, if you like the fried vegetables, corn bread, and sweet potato pie, you can thank them."

"My mom makes delicious steamed vegetables," Alex Perez offers, "but I never had them fried."

"I guess your mom wasn't raised up in rural Alabama," Kayla replies. "When I was growing up, almost everything we ate was fried. I once had fried ice cream."

James turns toward me. "Do we have a case today, Doc?"

"I'm sorry James, we don't. Today we're going to talk about two law enforcement technologies the Sheriff's Department uses, drones and image recognition. First, we'll discuss drones. Let me introduce our guest speaker, Professor Greg Ziegler. Professor Ziegler spent his career working for various companies as they developed drone technology. He's the newest member of our college faculty and is working with the Sheriff's Department to help them make the best use of drones."

"Thanks, professor." Greg approaches the speaker's lectern. "Has anyone here ever used a drone? Adiva, I know you have. Anyone else."

"I got one for my birthday, last year," Judy responds. "I fly it over the lake by my house. My little brother once got hold of it, attached a camera, and peeked into one of our neighbor's open windows. My parents were apologizing for a week."

Alex is next to speak. "Mr. Granderson, who owns the farm where my parents work, showed me an application called Agri-Drone. He uses it to identify areas that need nutrients, insecticides, fungicides, or other treatments. He then dispatches a second, larger drone, with a container attached, that shoots the appropriate chemicals into the affected areas."

Emanuel

"Anyone else?" Greg inquires. When no one speaks up, Greg gestures toward Adiva Fayed, who is sitting at one of the Tech Center's computers. "One of your Tech Squad members is going to help me with this presentation. Using drones, she was instrumental in helping you solve a recent case when a community theater actor was killed."

Adiva presses a few buttons on her computer, displaying a PowerPoint presentation on the Technology Center's screens. Greg proceeds to describe some of the uses law enforcement makes of drones. He explains how drones with camera mounts find missing persons, accident victims, and people lost in wooded and mountainous areas. They help locate bombs and toxic spills and can monitor the location of cars and trucks. "And," Greg says, "as Adiva showed you when solving the murder at the theater, drones can identify various plant types, such as marijuana."

"And poison mushrooms," Alex offers.

"And poison mushrooms," Greg repeats. "Police also deploy drones to find suspects trying to avoid detection by hiding in a building."

"But what good are these drones if the suspect is in a building?" Judy asks. "Do they have x-ray eyes, like Superman?"

"Can anyone answer that question?" I ask.

"Thermal cameras can sense heat emitted by animals and humans as well as detect their shape and motion," Alex answers. "Police can see a human being moving inside a building."

"Is all of this legal?" one of Tony's deputies inquires. "Don't we need warrants to use drones?"

"I can answer that," Tony replies. "We use the same guidelines applied to other searches. We can't point a drone-mounted camera into your home or property without a warrant, but we can video public areas. This is no different than traffic cameras. So, yes, if we want to use thermal cameras to peer into a building, we need a warrant."

"How do you control a drone?" another deputy asks. "I see some of my neighbors guide them from the ground, like they were flying a kite."

"Drones, and the devices we attach to them, such as cameras, may be manipulated using a computer, tablet, phone, or joy stick," Greg says. "Adiva operated the drones in your earlier case from right here in the Technology Center." Adiva smiles and raises her right arm and hand, extending two fingers in a victory sign.

The sheriff's deputies and students pose a few more questions, after which I step to the speaker's podium. "Thanks, Greg. Please feel free to stick around and enjoy some of the goodies on the snack table. Our next topic is image recognition. Alex has been working on an image recognition project. Alex, the floor is all yours." My nickname for Alex is *Mr. Enthusiasm.* Whenever I call for a volunteer, he's the first to raise his hand.

"Thanks, Doc." Alex brings up an application called MyImage, which displays on the left side of the Technology Center's computer screens. He then places a picture of himself, playing on the school baseball team, on the right side of the screen. "Now, as many of you know, I help my parents every week-end at our farmer's market booth. Mr. Granderson runs his drones, using the Agra-Drone software I mentioned earlier, to ensure that the fruits and vegetables are fresh. He'll call us if he wants something removed. He also flies drones over the market—."

"—To make sure no one is stealing?" Kayla suggests.

"He doesn't tell us that but, yeah, I think he's keeping everyone honest. Anyway, let's run the videos from last week's market and see if it can find the handsome devil shown in the picture on the right side of the screen."

"No modesty, there, Alex," Judy chides.

51

Emanuel

"None at all."

"Mr. Granderson gave me permission to use these images for this demonstration," Alex continues.

The MyImage software runs for about 15 seconds and stops when it finds Alex standing behind a table stacked with strawberries.

"Is it always that fast?" Kayla asks.

"It depends on how many images it has to scan. Law enforcement agencies use MyImage, and applications like it, to identify a suspect. They may have to compare a photo from multiple federal, state, and local databases. This can take hours, sometimes even days."

"Can it only identify photos of people?" Diego inquires.

"It can identify anything that can be displayed as an image file. The sheriff showed me a case from out west. Three guys about our age had gone hiking in the Colorado Rockies and didn't return. One of the boys had sent his father a photo attached to a text message, but it didn't say where he was. The local sheriff and park rangers used an imaging system to identify where the picture had been taken. They found the boys about a mile and a half from the location they identified, out of range of a cell tower, tired, hungry, but otherwise in good health."

The students ask Alex some additional questions, after which I dismiss the class.

"I'll just grab another slice of that sweet potato pie," Judy says, as she passes the snack table. "Thank goodness for grandmas. Without them we'd have nothing good to eat."

* * *

June 1968 – Long Binh Military Hospital
I try to open my eyes, but I can only see faint images. I hear what sounds like a woman's voice, but I don't understand what she's saying. "Fiorino," she later tells me I had murmured. Everything's a blur. I later learn that I had been dragged into the helicopter, gravely wounded, and brought to the hospital. I was placed in a corner along

52

with other men who, during triage, doctors and nurses called the expectant. This means we were expected to die. We were to be kept as comfortable as possible but given little, if any, medical attention. Triage policy states that medical teams and limited supplies are only used for those who are expected to live.

I guess I beat the odds. I'm still alive. I later learn that Private Fiorino wasn't so lucky. It takes me two more days, drifting in and out of consciousness, before I can stay awake and focus.

"Welcome back, soldier."

It's that same soft voice I heard when I first began to wake up, speaking in accented English. I try to raise up on my elbows but feel a sharp pain in my side and I fall back down on the bed.

"Don't try to move," the voice says. "You're alive, but you will have a long recovery. Right now, I have to change your bandages."

"Who are you?" I ask. I can focus clearly, now. She's a beautiful young woman, with the largest, almond shaped, almost pitch-black eyes I have ever seen.

"My name is Kim-Ly."

"Are you a nurse? You seem to be taking care of everyone in this room."

"Not exactly. I'm a translator. Many of the patients in this room are South Vietnamize soldiers—,"

"ARVN."

"Right, ARVN, The Army of the Republic of Vietnam."

"But you're changing my bandages. Isn't that what a nurse does?"

"It is, but, by regulation, nurses have to be American citizens. I'm Vietnamese so, officially, I'm a translator. I was trained as a nurse before the war and I spent time in Paris where I learned both French and English. My father was French."

Emanuel

"You spent time with your father in Paris?" I can see sadness in her eyes.

"No, my father was killed at Dien Bien Phu. I lived with my grandparents when I studied in Paris. When the hospital's head nurse found out I had medical training, she convinced the brass to let me perform nursing duties in this expectant room."

Over the next three days I'm feeling stronger and need less morphine for my pain. On the morning of the fourth day Kim-Ly tells me that I will be transferred to the hospital's recovery ward.

"Will you visit me?" I ask Kim-Ly, before I leave.

This beautiful young woman gently cradles my hand. "I will."

***

Current Day

As Gina Romano enters the Sun Coast Shores clubhouse for the meeting of the Self-Defense Club, she spies Steve Dombrowski at the snack table. "What did you mean by that crack at the Fourth of July planning meeting that *we'll take care of the rest*?" Gina asks.

"What the fu—," Steve immediately turns and sees Sandra Paulson with her video camera. "Sorry, I keep forgettin' our rule about being politically correct. What the blazes do you think I meant? Club members will patrol the community perimeter on the fourth, both inside and out. We'll be able to see anyone within shootin' range of our community firing off a gun."

Steve is the president of the Sun Coast Shores Self-defense Club. The club has two missions, self-defense education and the community watch program.

Gina is responsible for the self-defense classes. Over the years, she has shown her neighbors how to avoid situations that put them in harm's way, such as not using a bank's cash machine at night and suggesting to the women that they carry pepper spray and a police whistle in their purse. She and her committee are

54

currently planning a discussion of firearm safety in the home in anticipation of schools closing for the summer and the grandchildren visiting.

Gina had been the first female member of the club. It was because of Gina, and the three other female members, that the men had, reluctantly, begun watching their language, what Steve calls being *politically correct*. She doesn't have the heart to tell the men that, having three older brothers, she can match them, profanity for profanity, and then some. "Are we going to approach them, unarmed, and ask them, politely, to stop shooting?" Gina knows the word *unarmed* is a sensitive subject for community watch team members. The club's charter specifies that volunteers are not allowed to carry guns while on patrol. She also knows that she is one of the few who follows that rule.

In addition to being the Self-defense Club's president, Steve runs the community watch program.

"I meant that we'd keep watch on the perimeter and, if we see someone shootin', we'll immediately call the police."

"And how will we see them? They may be a mile or more from our perimeter. Can we see through buildings and trees?"

"I'm glad you asked that. This evening's speaker will address that very issue."

Steve mingles with the club members until the 7:00 meeting start time. He then moves behind the podium and raps his gavel. "Earlier this evening, Gina asked about my comment at the July Fourth planning meeting about how we're going to protect ourselves against our neighbors shooting their guns off. I'd like to ask Greg Ziegler, our newest member, to answer that question. I met Greg at the New Resident Social about two months ago. We got to talking about security and the problem we have with people in the neighboring community firing guns in the air. He came up with an answer. Greg."

"Thanks, Steve." Greg displays a PowerPoint presentation on the screen. "The answer to Gina's question is drones. Many of you own recreational drones." Greg turns toward Rick Sykes, who is sitting in the third row. "I know my friend Rick, here, says he bought a drone so his grandkids would have something to do when they visit, but we know better, don't we Rick?"

"You got me, Greg. My wife didn't want me to buy it. A toy for a seventy-two-year-old boy, she called it, but I know how to get to her. All I had to say was that it's for our grandkids when they visit, and she melted." The club members erupted in laughter. "She even suggested we buy two, since we have two grandchildren."

"Anyway," Greg continues, "We mount cameras on the drones and fly them over the neighboring community." Greg displays a video of drones hovering over a residential area. "If we see someone firing a gun, we'll call the cops."

"And tell them the best part," Steve says.

"We control the drones from our phones. We can enjoy the concert and fireworks on the main lawn at the same time we're doing our electronic patrolling. If we see someone shooting a gun, we simply dial 911."

"But what if the guy's stopped shooting before the cops get there?" Morris Greenberg asks. "The sheriff told us they can't just look at everyone's gun."

"We'll have a video from the camera on the drone," Greg replies. "The video should be enough for the sheriff to get a warrant for the gun. I'm handing out a sign-up sheet. Anyone who owns drones and wants to volunteer, let me have your name, telephone number, and email address."

Greg answers questions about drones and how they will be used during the July Fourth celebration, after which Dave adjourns the meeting.

Greg leaves the social hall and walks toward his car. A critical piece of his plan has fallen into place.

* * *

"Welcome to Rafael's Gun Shop," Rafael Rivera says, as he walks from behind the counter to greet the visitor who had just walked through the door. "And what can I do for you today?"

"I read the piece in the Sun Coast Shores Chronicle about you and your store. The picture shows you, —," the man pulls a newspaper article from his pocket, "—with a Remington Model 700 ADL rifle, pointing it into the air."

"That's the one I prefer," Rafael says. "My son and I use it to hunt deer."

"A friend convinced me to take up hunting, now that I'm retired. He owns that same rifle. He's going to let me use it when we go out next week. I told him I'd buy the bullets. I think he said I should buy a box of something called Remington AccuTip cartridges. Is that right? Do I also have to buy bullets?"

Rafael reaches behind the counter, retrieves a box of cartridges, and removes one of them, holding the bullet in his left hand and pointing with his right. "The cartridge is this long cylinder. It holds the bullet. When you buy cartridges, you also get the bullets."

"I get it. OK, I'll take that box."

Raphael returns the cartridge to the box and hands it to his customer. The man removes his wallet from his back pocket, pays in cash, and exits the store.

* * *

June 1968 – Long Binh Military Hospital

I had just finished lunch when I look up. My heart begins to pound. I place the journal I'm keeping under my pillow. My bed is at the end of a long hospital room. Every one of the other patients' eyes follow Kim-Ly as she walks toward me. Those who can sit up, do. "Hello again, soldier," she says. "You're looking a lot better than the last time I saw you."

Emanuel

"I'm feeling a lot better. I'm told I'll be up and around in no time."

"Do you need anything? Do you have books and magazines? I can bring them to you."

"I have all the reading material I need." I can see, from the look in Kim-Ly's eyes, that she's disappointed, possibly hurt, that I'm rejecting her offer of help. "Tell you what you can do. Bring the wheel chair over and take me outside. I could use a little fresh air." Kim-Ly's eyes light up. She walks toward the center of the room, where the wheelchairs are stacked. All eyes again follow her. She brings the chair to my bed, helps me into it, and wheels me out the door. We stop at a bench under a tree. She tells me about growing up in Saigon.

"I didn't have many friends. I'm half French, which meant none of the children in my village would talk to me. They called me 'con cái của kẻ thù'".

"What does that mean?"

"The literal translation is 'children of the enemy' and it was meant as a vile profanity. My mother made sure I went to school, so I didn't end up like most of the girls fathered by Frenchman; bar maids and prostitutes. I was only eight when my father died. When the French left Vietnam, my mother sent me to Paris to live with my grandparents. At first, they had a hard time accepting me but, over time, they became cordial, if not warm."

"Is your mother still alive."

A tear rolled down Kim-Ly's cheek. "She died while I was in Paris. Mother refused to leave Vietnam even though life was hard because she had a child by one of the hated French. By the time I finished school, the Americans and the ARVN were fighting the Communist north and the Viet Cong. My grandparents didn't want me to return. 'I must go back,' I told them. 'Vietnam is my home.'"

"'You have your father's stubbornness," my grandfather said, as he saw me off at the airport.

I tell her about my life growing up in Oconomowoc, Wisconsin.

"Oco—," There's a puzzled look on her face. "My English is good," she says," but that's a hard one." We both laugh.

She listens when I tell her what I did as president of my high school Technology Club. The girls at my school ignored me. They preferred the football players, but Kim-Ly is interested when I tell her how we built a transistor ham radio. She even asks questions about the project. I tell her how I devoured books about computers and plan to go to college after the war and learn as much about them as I can.

It's getting dark and we look up to see the sun about to set. We have been sitting and talking for almost five hours, although it seems like minutes. "I probably missed dinner," I say. "You'd better get me back."

I sleep well that night.

"Sergeant, what the hell were you doing with that gook?" I wake suddenly to the sound of the lieutenant's angry voice only to see his face not two inches from mine.

"What are you talking about?"

"You know what I'm talking about." His voice grows even louder. "You spent the entire afternoon with that whore."

"You mean Kim-Ly."

"Yeah Kim— whatever her name is. If you're looking to get laid, you can do a lot better than that. I'm sure you can find a nurse, an American nurse, who can satisfy your needs. You don't need to hang around with one of them."

I'm now fully awake and use my elbows to pull myself to a sitting position. "All due respect sir, Kim-Ly is a Vietnamese translator and a friend."

"She's a gook, like all the other gooks. If it were up to me, those ARVN so called soldiers would be in their own hospitals and we wouldn't need those whores, oh, excuse me, translators."

Emanuel

The lieutenant turns quickly and storms toward the hospital ward door. As he is about to leave, he turns and glares at me. "Watch yourself, sergeant." I see him bolt through the door, grab a pack of those British cigarettes he likes, the ones with the distinctive red ring circling the filter, from his pocket. He pulls one out of the pack, and lights it.

* * *

<u>Current Day</u>

As Greg enters the room for the Photography Club meeting, a woman he guesses to be in her mid-sixties approaches him. "I haven't seen you here before," she says, glancing at his name tag, "Greg. Are you new to our club?"

"I am. I haven't used my camera in years but, now that I'm retired, I've decided to take up photography again."

"You say you're retired? What did you do?"

"I spent most of my career in information technology, the last ten years working for DJR."

"I don't think I ever heard of that company."

"Most people haven't. They're a small company that manufactures and supports recreational drones. I worked on the team that developed drones that they market for private use."

"Oh," the woman says. Greg could tell from the look on her face that she knows little, if anything, about drones.

"Does your wife share your interest in photography?"

Greg glances at the woman's left hand. He guesses why she asks that question. Over the years, he has learned not to answer. "So, what do we do at the Photography Club?"

The woman hesitates a moment. She realizes she isn't going to get an answer to her question. "We meet monthly. We have a guest speaker who demonstrates some photography function. This month, someone's talking about, I think it's called, photoshopping. We then have members display their photographs, usually by connecting their computers to the projection equipment, sometimes showing them in an album, you know, the old-fashioned way. They usually give technical details about their photos, like f-stops, megapixel, ISO sensitivity, things like that. I don't really understand that stuff, but I bet you do." The woman brushes back a strand of her hair and gently touches Greg's arm.

Greg breaks away from the woman when he sees Steve Dombrowski. He thanks the woman who had welcomed him and extends his hand to Steve. "It's good to see a familiar face."

"I didn't know you're a photographer," Steve says.

"I don't know if you'd call me a photographer. I own a twenty-year-old Cannon I haven't used in over fifteen years."

"Then you've come to the right place. Many of us are in the same boat. We're taking up a hobby we enjoyed earlier in our lives but, somehow, abandoned." The two men take seats in the fourth row of chairs.

Christine MacBride, the Photography Club's vice-president grabs the microphone. "OK, let's get started. Sandra usually runs this meeting, but she's busy recording everything we say and do," she says, pointing to the club president, standing on the side of the room, a video camera resting on her shoulder. "I believe most of you know my husband, Dennis. He's the Photography Club's past-president and, since retiring from the Army, has become an expert in photoshopping. Dennis."

Greg sits up straight. He wants to leave but it would be awkward stepping over the four people who are sitting between him and the aisle and then walking the almost fifty feet to the meeting room door.

"Thanks, Babe," Dennis says. "I don't know if you'd call me an expert, but I've learned a lot about the subject in the last six months, since I bought myself photoshopping software for Christmas. Can anyone tell me what photoshopping is?"

A man toward the back of the room stands up. "It's where I can take a picture of my wife, here," he says, pointing at the plump woman next to him, "and place her head on a picture of some super model in a bikini." Some of the men laugh. Every woman in the room, including the man's wife, glares at him.

I don't envy this guy when he gets home, Greg thinks.

"Photoshopping gives us the ability to alter a picture or video." Dennis displays two images, side by side. "Take a look at these snapshots of a beautiful sunset over our main lake. The one on the left is ruined because of that trash can at the bottom. The image on the right is the same photo, but I've removed the trash can."

"Can I remove wrinkles from my face?" a woman in the fifth row asks.

"You sure can."

"Sign me up."

"Hey, maybe I can wear my speedo bathing suit and have this photoshop thing take off a few pounds, like maybe fifty."

"Sorry, Andy, even photoshopping can't work that kind of magic."

After the laughter dies down, Dennis displays a grainy picture from the local newspaper. After he pushes a few buttons on the computer, the image becomes crystal clear. "I can also change part of the picture." Dennis shows a photo of a man holding a baseball in his right hand. A few maneuvers with the mouse, and the baseball is in the man's left hand.

"And finally, what I consider the most important feature. I can replace one image with another." A snapshot displays showing Dennis, standing in a boat, holding a fish that appears to be about eight inches long. "This is a picture my friend, Rob, took two weeks ago on the Fishing Club's charter in the Gulf." He then displays a second photo which looks exactly like the first, except that the fish is close to four feet long. "And this is the image I show everyone when they ask me how I did on my last fishing trip." There is loud laughter and some applause from the meeting attendees. "And that," he says, "is a brief explanation of photoshopping."

Dennis spends the next 30 minutes showing other features, such as adding or adjusting color, inserting text, and creating animation.

After Dennis's presentation, three of the club members display photos and videos they had taken on recent vacations to Indonesia, Malaysia, and Nepal. Greg feigns attention to the member's photos and videos. He's glad that he hadn't left the meeting. Another piece of his plan falls into place.

* * *

September 1968 – Long Binh Military Hospital

I spend three months recovering in the Long Binh Military Hospital. I want to get back into action but that's out of the question. I lost a kidney and my leg muscles will never be 100%. The guys in my hospital ward ask when I will be going through the rehab exercises I need to strengthen my leg. They say it's because they want to help me. I think they have other motives. You see, Kim-Ly often visits me at the rehab center.

I figure I'll be sent home. After all, the rehab facilities are much better stateside. Most guys can't wait to get away from this war. I have mixed feelings. Yeah, I miss my family, but I have a reason to stay.

It's a hot, humid afternoon, which, basically, describes every day in-country. By now I'm on crutches so I can get to the mess hall on my own. I get to talking with some of the guys who run the base's computer facilities. Over the next two weeks we talk computers every day. I realize I know more about these machines from the books I've read than they do with their college degrees. It isn't long before

Emanuel

I'm assigned to the computer room. Even with my missing kidney and bum leg, the brass sees I could help them keep their machines humming.

* * *

Current Day

Greg Ziegler wakes suddenly. He's having that dream again, the one in the Vietnamese village. After over fifty years, he still can't shake it. He pours himself a cup of tea and turns on the television. Sometimes these old movies help him fall back to sleep. Not tonight. He decides to get some fresh air. He's been walking for approximately fifteen minutes when he enters the two-mile footpath that circumvents the community's signature lake. It's a clear night. The moon casts its light over the water's ripples. He wishes he'd brought his camera. This would make a beautiful shot for the next Photography Club meeting.

He had walked approximately one-hundred yards when he approaches a man, sitting on a bench on the grass bordering the lake, tossing a line from a fishing pole into the water.

"Anything biting?" Greg asks.

"So far, nothing, but I'm a patient man."

Greg has one of those faces with no real distinguishing features. For most of his life people encounter him three or four times before they remember him. Once, when he was eight years' old, he got lost in a department store. His mother, father, aunt, and uncle looked for him for over an hour. Finally, his uncle saw him in a remote dressing room, but was about to turn and leave when Greg yelled, "Uncle Jack!" and ran toward him. Even an eight-year-old could sense that it took a few seconds for Jack Ziegler to recognize his own nephew. For most of his life he had cursed his easily forgettable face. Tonight, it played to his advantage.

"Isn't this an odd time to be fishing?" Greg asks.

64

"Not really. I'm a nocturnal being. I'm often awake most of the night and rest during the day. It's one of the advantages of being retired. I can sleep when I'm tired, not when the world says I should. Do you fish?"

"I don't, but I think I might try it. It looks so relaxing."

"It is. Tell you what, why don't you join me right here, on this bench, on Thursday. I plan to be here at 9:30, during the community's July 4th celebration. I'm going to fish and watch the fireworks. I'd welcome the company."

"Thanks, but I'll pass. I plan to watch the concert on the lawn."

"OK, suit yourself."

Greg turns and begins walking back home. He is overcome by a feeling of euphoria. Another piece of his puzzle falls into place.

* * *

October 1968 – Long Binh Military Base

"Need that jeep, again, Sarge?" Harry Choy says. Harry, and the guys in the motor pool, know what I'm doing, and they arrange to get me a jeep when I need it.

"I can't let the Lieutenant know where I'm going. I think he hates all Vietnamese, even those we're fighting for."

"It's not just Vietnamese," Harry says. "My family's been in America since my great grandfather helped build the transcontinental railroad after the civil war, but the lieutenant still treats me with disdain. In his eyes, if you look like me, you're the enemy."

It takes me about an hour to get to Kim-Ly's place. She usually prepares dinner when we're together. I'm getting used to her cooking, a combination of Vietnamese and French dishes. Once, I borrowed some food from the mess hall and prepared meat loaf, mashed potatoes, and green beans. Kim-Ly was gracious as we ate, but I could sense that she did not care for American dishes.

I had decided to show her the journal I'm keeping. She appears a little embarrassed when she sees the part about her, but she smiles and puts her arm around me and rests her head on my shoulder.

"I love you, too," see purrs.

"I'm going to be away for about two weeks," she says later that evening, as I'm about to leave.

"A little R&R?" I ask. "Can I come along?"

"Not exactly. I'm working with Project Care, a Vietnamese Civilian Organization that provides medical services to local villages. Your base hospital has given us medical supplies and equipment. I'll be going to two villages, Phu Coung and Gia Binh."

I'll miss Kim-Ly, but it's only two weeks. It will pass quickly, and I'll see her again, or so I thought.

. . .

Current Day

My wife, Deb, and Marie Maggio are packing their offerings for this evening's July 4th celebration.

"Are all your dishes homemade?" I ask Marie.

"Sure are, Lionel. My mother brought these recipes from Italy and taught me how to make everything from scratch."

Deb has prepared her mother's Ambrosia salad recipe, drained cans of fruit, maraschino cherries, and mandarin oranges, mixed with sour cream and coconut. Tony and I are sitting in my family room waiting for the women to complete their preparations.

"We're ready to go," Marie says. We place chairs and blankets in the back of my golf cart, and we're off. Marie and Deb hold the bowls containing the food on their laps. Tony cradles two bottles of wine, plastic utensils, paper plates, and cups. I'm in the driver's seat.

"You maxing this thing out?" Tony asks.

"Yup," I reply. "If I have the wind to my back, we can hit fifteen miles an hour, sometimes eighteen, if a hurricane's approaching."

I drop the two women off near the tables where everyone is depositing their food. Tony and I drive to the designated parking area. We return, carrying the chairs, blanket, wine, utensils, paper plates, and cups to the great lawn. We find our wives and settle in.

"I'll be back in a few minutes," I say. "I've got to check on the crew."

I walk toward the jumbo screen that will be used to project the concert.

"Hey, Professor," a young man, wearing the polo shirt uniform of the Tampa Bay Cable Company, says as I approach. "We really appreciate the help your students are providing in getting everything set up. We weren't happy when our bosses told us we would be working with some kids. We figured we'd be doing little more than baby sitting and it would take twice as long to get the job done. We were wrong. As soon as we met your students, the one over there," he said, pointing toward Diego, "organized the others and got them started on their assignments."

"That's Diego, the leader of the pack."

"They helped us solve some problems we ran into getting this screen hooked up. You've obviously taught them well."

"Thanks," I say, glancing at the name on the man's shirt, "Rob. Glad we could help."

I glance over at the Tech Squad working with the cable company team. I'm proud of them. When I return to Deb, Tony, and Marie, the chairs are open, and utensils, plates, cups, and wine bottles are spread on the blanket. We return to the food tables and pile our plates with more than we really need. We return to our chairs, pour wine, which we place next to our chairs, and, with plates in our laps, prepare for our evening of good food, beverages, and music.

It's just past 8:15. The sun is setting over the horizon and the jumbo screen displays the opening credits of the Boston Pops Orchestra's July 4th concert.

Emanuel

"Remember, back at Franklin, we used to come to these outdoor concerts, lay on the blanket, and stare at the sky as we listened to the music," I say, gently taking Deb's hand.

"Don't even think about it, bub," Deb replies, smiling. "Forty years ago, we were young and limber. Now, getting down and lying on the blanket would be fun, getting up, not so much."

We enjoy the evening's performance. As the orchestra begins the finale, the 1812 Overture, I glance around. Most of my neighbors are aiming their phones at the fireworks. Some are looking down at their screens. I get my phone and decide to take photos of my neighbors taking pictures.

...

September 1968 – Long Binh Military Base

When I enter the Computer Room, I see the veins in the lieutenant's neck bulging. "Goddammit, this can't be right!" He's standing in front of a computer terminal holding a printout in one hand and a cigarette in the other.

"It is, sir," the sergeant in charge of the Computer Room says, "We printed the results—."

The lieutenant doesn't wait for the sergeant to finish his sentence. "This says my kill ratio is only 8-1. I know it's higher than that. Three days ago, we raided a VC village and killed at least fifty of those gooks."

"And you lost eight men," the sergeant says.

The lieutenant whirls around and storms out of the room.

"What's that all about?" I ask.

"Field officer's evaluations are heavily skewed to kill ratios," the sergeant replies, "which is the number of enemy killed compared to the number we lose. The brass wants at least 10-1. The guys who get promoted show as high as 12 or 13-1. Over the last three months, the lieutenant's numbers are down. His career's in jeopardy. He'll do whatever it takes to get his numbers up."

68

Murder By The Lake

The next morning, the sergeant is in a particularly good mood. "He's out of our hair for a few days."

"Who?"

"That damn lieutenant who wants to get his kill ratio up and blames us when we show him the printout. But now he's out in the field, again."

The sergeant shows me the printout of the supplies and equipment ordered for the raid, which began at dawn. As I read the details of the lieutenant's plans I freeze, drop the paper I'm holding, and bolt from the room. I could be court-martialed for what I'm about to do. I don't care.

I run to the motor pool, grab a map and a jeep, and speed off. I know how to get off the post without being spotted. They'll be after me. I don't care.

* * *

Current Day

Peter Morales rounds a bend in the grassy area bordering Sun Coast Shores' big lake. His head pounds as he steers his riding lawn mower. The night before he had stayed up late, drinking and watching the fireworks. He had seen the signs and heard the radio and TV announcements, in both English and Spanish, telling people not to fire guns in the air. But, what the heck, there were no cops around, so why not. He didn't remember falling asleep. When the alarm on his watch sounded, he found himself lying in the grass, soaked from the night's dew. He would have hell to pay when he got home that night but, now, he had to get to work. His job with Real Green Maintenance, managing landscaping for all those rich folks in their gated communities, paid well and provided benefits for Gloria and their three, soon to be four, kids.

He doesn't see the body in front of the bench. He is almost thrown from the seat on his mower when he hits the figure lying, face down, in the grass, with a fishing rod at his side. *Did I hurt someone*, he thinks? His first

69

impulse is to keep going and ignore the obstacle in front of him. He glances up and spies two people jogging along the path that circumvents the lake. They wave, and he waves back. It doesn't appear that they see the body, but they see him. He can't leave unnoticed. He has only one choice. He calls his supervisor. *What will happen now,* he thinks? *Dios mío, what will happen now?*

"What the hell did you do?" his supervisor asks when he arrives, about twenty minutes later. "This man looks dead. Did you kill him?"

"I don't think so. He was lying there when I came around that curve. I couldn't stop before I hit him."

It takes only fifteen minutes for Sheriff Tony Maggio and two of his deputies to arrive.

"Did I do this?" Peter asks, as he sits under a tree, his legs pulled up almost to his chin, and both of his hands holding his bowed head.

The sheriff kneels next to him. "You didn't do anything but hit a man who was already dead. We'll know more when the coroner examines him, but, from the state of rigor, it appears he died four or five hours ago, maybe more."

Peter breathes a sigh of relief. "How did he die?"

"From what I can see," the sheriff says, "from multiple gunshot wounds."

* * *

"We got a case today?" Diego asks, as my students mingle around the snack table. Tony had volunteered to bring the goodies.

"These are delicious," Judy says. "Where can we buy them?"

"These are home made by the greatest Italian chef I know, my wife, Marie," Tony replies. "You can't buy them in any store and, to answer Mr. Rivera's question, yes, we have a case. This one's close to home, the shooting death of Dennis MacBride, a resident of the Sun Coast Shores community, where your professor, here, lives."

"Is he a suspect?" Alex chides.

"Gee, I hope not," I reply. "And if I am, I've got an alibi."

"He does," Tony says. "Mr. MacBride died three days ago, on July 4th. Our medical examiner estimates time of death as somewhere between 9:00 and 11:00 PM. Your professor and I were enjoying a firework's display at the time."

"The sheriff as your alibi," Judy observes. "I guess that's as good as it gets."

Tony is sitting at a computer terminal. The students and the sheriff's deputies sit at individual terminals, looking at screens positioned on the Sheriff Department's Technology Center walls. Tony displays a series of images.

"What we know so far," Tony begins, displaying an image of the victim's head, with the eye socket and part of his skull torn away, lying on the Medical Examiner's table, "is that Mr. MacBride died from gunshot wounds from bullets shot from a rifle. Two bullets entered his skull and one went through the right eye."

"Gross," Judy says, turning her head away.

"You'll have to get used to that, young lady," a deputy replies, "if you're going to study crime investigation."

"How do you know the bullets came from a rifle, and not a handgun?" Alex asks.

"Rifles use different types of bullets than handguns," Tony replies.

"Do we know how Mr. MacBride was shot?" James asks.

"We don't," Tony responds. "The bullets entered his head from a steep downward angle. The shooter would have to be standing close to the victim, shooting downward. This is possible with a hand gun but awkward with a rifle, even if Mr. McBride was sitting on the bench."

"I think I have a way of finding out what happened," James says. "Do you have photographs of the crime scene?"

"We do," the sheriff answers, displaying pictures the crime scene technicians had taken.

"Then let's boot up the Photomesh software we used to help solve Mr. Agnew's murder. Also, I'm working on a project with Kayla, where we combine images from Photomesh with Simsoft simulation and animation software. Kayla, could you access Simsoft?"

"I sure can."

It takes James approximately fifteen minutes to re-create the crime scene using Photomesh. "Now, let's assume Mr. MacBride was sitting on the bench when he was shot. Kayla, please show the scene using Simsoft."

"Using the 3-D image James created of the crime scene," Kayla says, "I add a man approaching the victim, holding the rifle butt above his head, and shooting. The sheriff is right. Even with Mr. McBride on the bench, the shooter would have had to stand in front of him and hold the rifle at an awkward angle for the bullets to impact him as they did. Not very likely."

"Any other options, techy guys?" Tony asks.

Kayla removes the shooter from the animation. "The bullet could have come from above," she says.

"But how?" Judy asked.

"From one of those son-of-a-bitches shooting his damn gun in the air," a deputy replies. "The killer could have been in the neighboring community celebrating the 4th of July. What goes up, must come down. These bullets came down on this poor guy's head."

The door to the lab opens and Madilyn Grayson, the county's Crime Scene Investigation Unit Supervisor, hands Tony a file. "We were able to get a partial fingerprint from the bullet fragment that entered his eye. The two bullets that entered his head shattered on impact. Because the third bullet went through soft tissue,

72

we were able to get the print. It matches one registered with the county for a gun shop owner, Rafael Rivera. I did some digging and found a recent newspaper article about Mr. Rivera and his gun shop, which shows him holding a Remington 700. The bullet is the kind used in that type of rifle. He lives in the community next to Sun Coast Shores. He might very well be the shooter."

Diego's face turns white and he slumps in his chair. "That— can't be, it just can't be." Everyone can see the agony in Diego's face. "Rafael Rivera is my father."

* * *

It's been four days since the county's CSI team identified Rafael Rivera as the prime suspect in Dennis MacBride's death. I arrange to meet with Rafael and his attorney, and arrive early to talk with Tony, first. "My students have a special request for this week's Tech Squad workshop. We'd like to talk about the July 4th shooting in my community. You've arrested the father of one of my students. Diego says his father never left home that evening."

"The evidence is pretty damning," Tony says. "His fingerprint is on the bullet. We also have a video showing him in a group of July 4th revelers. He's pointing a rifle in the air and appears to be shooting. We've verified that the video was taken around the time of McBride's death and the bullet could have come from the type of rifle Mr. Rivera owns. Our forensic specialists have verified that the bullets shot into the air from that rifle could have traveled into your community and struck Mr. MacBride."

"Where did you get the video?"

"From one of your residents," Tony replies, as he fumbles through his notes. "I'm sure we have this information on our computer, somewhere, but I'm still stuck with the old ways, notebook and pencil. Ah, here it is, Greg Ziegler. Isn't he the guy who talked to the Tech Squad about drones?"

Emanuel

"He is. How did he get a video?"

"With a drone. Your Self Defense Club flew drones over the neighborhoods surrounding your community, took pictures of those idiots shooting their guns in the air, and reported it to us in real time."

"Is that even legal?"

"The law is still catching up with technology, but courts have said that private citizens can take pictures in public places. We sent squad cars out but didn't catch anyone in the act. We've arrested four people identified from Mr. Ziegler's video, including Mr. Rivera. Our DA isn't sure if these photos will hold up in court, but she's going to try."

"The Tech squad would still like to take another look. I've excused Diego from class, so he can be with his family, and I have a favor to ask."

"Whatever you need."

"Can we get a warrant for all of the Self Defense Club's videos? That could give us a better idea of what took place in the surrounding community."

"I'll get that warrant. We can always use your students' help."

* * *

"I understand that you and your Tech Squad might be able to help me," Rafael Rivera says as he and I, along with his lawyer, Matthew Hanley, meet in the Sheriff Department's Interview Room.

"We're going to try. The sheriff tells me they have two pieces of evidence against you, your fingerprint on the bullet and a picture of you shooting a rifle in the air within the time frame when Mr. MacBride was killed. Can you explain either of these pieces of evidence?"

"I can probably explain the bullet. I handle them all the time in my shop, showing them to customers and demonstrating firearms at safety classes we hold. It's possible I held it, placed it back in the box, and sold it to a customer, who could have shot the rounds that killed

74

Mr. MacBride. I have a video system in the store and training room. You can see how often I hold bullets."

Attorney Hanley bends forward in his chair. "Even if that's the case," he injects, "the prosecution will argue that the killer's fingerprint should also be on the bullet."

"I don't know," Rafael responds, "maybe he wore gloves."

"How about the video?" I ask.

"I can't answer that," Rafael replies. "Anyone who has taken a safety class at my shop knows how adamant I am about the dangers of randomly firing guns. I don't even like to be out on holidays, when I know my neighbors are going to drink and be reckless. I spent the evening at home, watching TV with Diego and my wife. I didn't do this, but I don't know how to prove it."

Attorney Hanley and I walk to the parking lot together. "I won't sugarcoat it, professor. I don't want to take this to a jury. The evidence is damning, and, with people in the community wanting to pin this on someone, it may be all the prosecution needs. This is a case where the suspect may be assumed guilty unless we can prove him innocent."

* * *

As Tony and I enter the Sheriff's Department's Technology Center I sense a somber atmosphere. No one brought snacks and there is no lighthearted banter. The students are sitting at their terminals, not saying a word. It's more like a wake than a Tech Squad workshop.

I look up when I hear the door open. "Diego, you don't have to be here. You should be with your family."

"Professor," the formal word, professor, rather than the students' usual Prof or Doc, tells me everything I needed to know about Diego's mood, "my dad's life is on the line. I want to help. I need to help."

"OK, we welcome your input."

Emanuel

During last week's Tech Squad meeting, when Tony identified Diego's father as the prime suspect, Adiva was quiet. She focused on the information being presented and took a few notes. It doesn't surprise me that Adiva, the *Quiet One*, analyzed the situation and is now the first to speak.

"The best way to try to clear Mr. Rivera," she begins, "is to see how Mr. Ziegler's video shows Mr. Rivera shooting the rifle when he says he was home with his family. James, can you bring up the video?"

James displays the eight-second segment showing Rafael shooting the rifle. The class watches it run five times. Suddenly, Judy picks her head up from her phone. If I didn't know better, I would have thought she hadn't been paying attention. I know better.

"Did you see those flickers?" she asks.

"What flickers?" Alex replies.

"At the beginning of the video and, again, as he raises the rifle."

"I see it," Alex says.

Kayla leans toward the screen. "Me too. What does it mean?"

"I'll tell you what it means," James says. "Sheriff, if you send this video for analysis, I think you'll find that Mr. Rivera's image was photoshopped into the scene. He was never there."

"We don't have photo analysis equipment here," Tony replies, "but the state and the feds do. I'll ship it off right away."

"Where did the picture come from?" Judy asks.

"Probably, from the newspaper," Diego responds. "The Sun Coast Shores Chronicle ran a series about local businesses. One article was about my dad's shop."

"Photos in newspapers are pretty grainy," one of the deputies says. "The picture in the video is sharp."

"Photo enhancing software can work miracles," James replies. He accesses the newspaper's web site, finds the

76

grainy picture used in the article and, with a few key strokes, the photo looks exactly like the one in the video.

As James is talking, Kayla's fingers begin to glide across her keyboard. The Simsoft application displays on one of the screens. "Animation technology allows us to manipulate the photoshopped image." She selects Rafael's picture that James had just enhanced and is able to duplicate the image on the video.

It's my turn to help with the case. I display three new videos.

"These were all taken by my community's Self Defense Club, using drone mounted cameras, the evening of July 4th. Alex, at one of our workshops you talked about image recognition. Let's see if you can find another image of the same scene, at the same time, on another video. This will confirm our photoshopping theory."

"I should be able to do that, Doc," Alex says. "There's a bodega in the background with people walking by, entering, and leaving. I'll look for an exact match."

I can see Diego's mood changing as he senses we're clearing his father.

It takes approximately fifteen minutes for Alex to find an exact image match. Two people are approaching the bodega, one is leaving, and one is standing outside, smoking. My students stare at the screen the entire time, silent, and hardly moving. "There it is!" Alex exclaims, raising his fist in the air, "the exact same scene. Mr. Ziegler's video shows Mr. Rivera and, in the second video, he's not there." The entire class appears to exhale with relief at the same time.

"We'll take the picture from the video and find these witnesses," Tony injects.

"What about the fingerprint," Kayla asks?

"I've reviewed surveillance video from Mr. Rivera's store," Tony replies. "Just like he said, he handles bullets all the time. The shooter probably bought a box after Mr. Rivera handled it."

I can sense the class's mood lightening, but I'm concerned. I remember Attorney Hanley's comments about people wanting to blame someone for Dennis's death. Regardless of evidence showing the doctored tape, I'm afraid they'll want to convict Raphael. Juries have been known to send innocent defendants to jail. I'd like to find out what really happened. "Right now, all we know is that someone, probably Greg Ziegler, doctored the tape. I'm assuming he's the killer. Let's see if we can find out how and why he did it."

Alex sits straight up. "I think I got it!" he shouts, "at least the *how* part. Remember, at the last Tech Squad meeting, Mr. Ziegler asked if anyone was familiar with drones and I talked about Agri-Drone."

"I remember what you said," Adiva responds. "Agri-Drone shoots chemicals into affected areas of the farm."

"If a drone can hold a chemical container and shoot liquid into a field," Alex continues, "why can't it hold a gun and shoot bullets?"

* * *

The following week the Tech Squad meeting is back to normal. James supplies the snacks, peanut and pumpkin muffins, roasted almonds, and egg rolls.

"Did you make these?" Kayla asks.

"I wanted to, but my mom nixed the idea, something about my cooking skills, or lack thereof, and not wanting to destroy our kitchen, so, I bought them."

"We've got a lot to talk about today," I say, "and I want to introduce a special guest, Mr. Rafael Rivera."

Rafael stands. Diego turns toward his father. I see the pride on Diego's face. "I want to thank everyone in this class," Rafael begins. "Diego says you helped get me out of jail. I hope, some day, I can do something for each of you."

"Just make sure Diego keeps coming to class," Judy replies. "He's our leader."

Now, I see the pride in Rafael's face.

Tony stands and speaks to the class. "I'm sure you want to know how the case played out. We arrested Greg Ziegler for the murder of Dennis MacBride. Our warrants of Mr. Ziegler's financial records show he purchased a Remington Model 700 rifle online. Surveillance videos from Mr. Rivera's store confirm that he handled bullets when he showed them to Mr. Ziegler, who then bought them. We searched Mr. Ziegler's home and found a half-empty box of bullets, rubber gloves, which we assume he used when loading the rifle, a thermal-camera, and multiple drones, one of which can hold two devices. We assume Mr. Ziegler mounted the camera and a rifle on the drone. Using thermal-technology, he found Mr. MacBride, used the camera to aim the rifle, and shot."

"But how did he know Mr. MacBride would be at the lake that evening?" Judy asks.

"I can answer that," I respond. "I was at a recent Community Association meeting planning our July 4th celebration. Mr. Ziegler also attended that meeting. Mr. MacBride said he wasn't going to attend the festivities because he would be on his favorite bench around our main lake, fishing and watching the fireworks. All that Mr. Ziegler had to do was run his drone around the lake, looking for Mr. MacBride at the time the fireworks began. He may already have known where Mr. MacBride's bench was."

"Can we prove that he triggered the shot?" James asks.

"We can," I reply. "When the fireworks began, I took pictures of my neighbors photographing the display. Most of my photos show people aiming their phones upward, but five people were looking down at their screens. Greg Ziegler was one of these five. The other four were also Self-Defense Club members guiding their drones."

Emanuel

Tony continues. "We got a warrant to search Mr. Ziegler's smart phone's Internet Service Provider account, which recorded everything he did on his device that evening. When the fireworks began, he steered his drone over the lake and then moved it back over the surrounding community. We assume he shot Mr. MacBride during the display, knowing that the noise would drown out the shots."

"But what about a motive?" Alex asks. "What was Mr. Ziegler's motive for killing Mr. MacBride?"

* * *

September 1968 – Phu Coung, Vietnam

The helos land in a field just outside the village of Phu Coung. The lieutenant jumps out when the aircraft is still six feet off the ground. He bolts forward about five yards and turns toward the three helicopters, facing the one hundred and fifty-two men of C Company as they quickly jump to the ground.

"You have your orders," the lieutenant shouts. "This village is awash with VC sympathizers who hide enemy soldiers and weapons." He knows this isn't true. He doesn't care. "We go in, guns blazing, and neutralize everything and everyone."

"What about women and children?" a young private asks.

"You heard my order, son. We neutralize everyone. Now move, and don't forget body count. I need body count for my report."

* * *

I floor the jeep's gas pedal and race down the dirt road outside of the compound, placing the map on the steering wheel. I can't afford to take the time to stop and get my bearings. I read the map and drive at the same time. It appears to be about 60 km to Phu Coung. With luck, I will be there in two to three hours. My whole body is shaking as I steer around the ruts in the roadway. I try not to think about why I'm doing this.

80

* * *

Corporal Rick Baldwin leads the first squad as they enter the village. An old man and a teenage boy are sitting in front of a straw hut. They attempt to rise as they see the American soldiers. The corporal lifts his rifle and shoots. These two people are the first of four hundred and twenty-six villagers who die that day.

The corporal looks at Private First-Class Willie Rasmussen. Willie's jaw drops, and his eyes are wide open. The kid's new in country, the corporal thinks. He'll get over it. "Shoot, you son-of-a bitch. You know our orders." The private lifts his flame thrower and torches the hut. What appear to be a man and a woman run out, their tattered clothing in flames. The corporal again lifts his rifle and fires. He then takes a pad and pen from his pocket and notes, four.

The corporal sees a group of three old men, two women, one pregnant, and four children huddled in front of a hut. He slams his rifle into the old man's head and orders the villagers to move closer together. He steps back about five feet, aims his rifle, and shoots. Nine more to add to the lieutenant's body count, he thinks.

The lieutenant has just killed his eighth villager. He lights up a cigarette and has taken three deep drags when he spots her, a beautiful young woman, standing in front of three children, appearing to be protecting them. She looks healthier and cleaner than her fellow countrymen, and dresses better. This one's mine, he thinks. He flips his cigarette to the ground, grabs the woman, and knocks her to her knees. She fights but is no match for the muscular man as he rapes her. When he finishes, he pulls his pistol from its holster and shoots the woman and then the children.

For the remainder of the morning, the men of C company move through the village, shooting at will and torching every hut. Four people, three men and a woman, run into

81

the thick foliage when the carnage begins. They're the only survivors of the massacre.

"Move out," the lieutenant orders at about 1:30 in the afternoon, as he points to the helos. "Let's get the hell out of here."

* * *

When I arrive at the village, I see the slaughter that has occurred. The lieutenant calls the huts that have been burned to the ground hooches. The people who live there call them home. Bodies, many of them children, lay strewn over the ground. I approach an old woman hovering behind a tree. Kim-Ly had taught me some Vietnamese. "Y tá? (nurse)?" I ask.

"Đằng kia (Over there)," the woman says, pointing to a clump of trees approximately fifty feet away. I run toward where she's pointing and see three dead children, and then throw up. Kim-Ly's lifeless body is lying in a pool of blood, a cigarette butt, with a red ring circling the filter, not two inches from her left foot. I run to her, cradle her head in my lap, and don't move for what seems like an eternity. That son-of-a bitch. He needs to get his kill ratio up, so he attacks Phu Coung, a defenseless village. He will be able to report a heavy body count without losing a man.

I'm numb as I drive back to the base, my uniform drenched in Kim-Ly's blood, fully expecting to be arrested. I don't care. Everyone in the motor pool stares at me when I arrive. I exit the jeep and walk toward the computer room. Nothing happens.

Two days later I'm brought up under an Article 15, non-judicial punishment, for taking the jeep and leaving the post without authorization. I'm reduced in rank, given an honorable discharge, and sent home. I'm told I was shown leniency because I had almost died from my wounds during the earlier raid on Bien Hoa. The army doesn't even object when I receive veteran's benefits to complete my education.

* * *

82

Oconomowoc, Wisconsin - 1971

Over the next two years I learn why I got off so easily. I was a witness to the aftermath of the slaughter in Phu Coung. At the time, the 1968 My Lai massacre was coming to light. The army didn't want another blemish on its record. Phu Coung was swept under the rug. No action was taken against the officers and men who carried out the massacre. That son-of-a bitch Lieutenant Dennis MacBride ruined my life.

* * *

"I can answer Alex's question about a motive," I respond. "When the sheriff searched Ziegler's home, he found an old, faded journal which told a tragic story. Ziegler was a sergeant in MacBride's, then Lieutenant MacBride's, unit in Vietnam. It appears that Ziegler was in love with a Vietnamese nurse/translator, Kim-Ly. Lieutenant MacBride ordered an attack on a Vietnamese village where Kim-Ly was serving as a visiting nurse. Kim-Ly was raped and killed during that raid. There was a cigarette butt by Kim-Ly's body. Ziegler recognized the butt by the distinctive red ring on the filter. There was no doubt in Ziegler's mind that MacBride raped and killed his lover.

"Ziegler never married. I suspect he silently harbored a broken heart throughout his life.

"When we discovered this connection between the two men, we dug a little deeper. The president of our community Photography Club took videos of recent South Coast Shores events. The sheriff got warrants for those videos. He and I spent hours watching them, looking for segments that showed Ziegler, to see what we could learn about him." At this point I pause, waiting for the response I know will come.

"Doc, did you really spend hours?" Alex asks, smiling.

"OK, Alex, you got me. With Alex's help, we used the MyImage software to search for Ziegler's image. The videos told us a great deal about the man. Last March, after living in Sun Coast Shores for only a few weeks, he went to a meeting of the Military Veterans club. When he encountered MacBride at the refreshments table, he dropped his cake and coffee and walked out of the room.

"He went to a subsequent meeting where community members discussed using drones to monitor the surrounding areas to find people shooting guns in the air during the fourth of July celebration. He was also at a gathering which demonstrated how to enhance, animate, and photoshop pictures. The videos show that Ziegler avoided questions about family and was cold to women in the community who tried to befriend him. I don't think Ziegler ever forgave MacBride."

"We searched his financial records," Tony says, "and found that he purchased the same rifle Mr. Rivera showed him in the store, on the Internet.

"The sheriff confiscated Ziegler's computer," I continue. "It shows he enhanced and animated the picture and photoshopped it into the video he gave us. The DA sees no problem convicting Ziegler with the evidence he has."

"Did you find the rifle?" James asks.

"Not yet," Tony says. "We suspect he had the drone release it over the lake. Our divers are searching for it now."

Diego stands, tears in his eyes, "Thank you, my friends."

Judy can't help ending our session on a lighter note. "So, D, will you ask your Aunt Isabella to go light on the salsa next time you bring snacks?" Everyone laughs, more a laugh of relief than from Judy's comment.

THE FAMILY JEWELS

The *Tech Squad* has taken a well-deserved late summer break after being instrumental in solving Dennis McBride's murder. Walking on campus the first week of the fall semester, I could see that my students had gained notoriety among their peers. They're always surrounded by a gaggle of their friends. They tell me the conversations inevitably turn to their cases. The school's Graphic Art Department and students in the English Department's Creative Writing seminar have created a *Tech Squad* comic, which they publish in the campus newspaper. Professor Jamison, a colleague of mine on the Science and Technology faculty, has been teaching a Video Game Development course for three years. This semester's project will be based on the *Tech Squad*'s exploits. My students are helping to develop their avatars. Diego wants his avatar wearing a cape and possessing super powers. They've become the big men and women on campus.

They hit the ground running the first week of class. They are on their way to another successful round of crime fighting when a case is thrown at them that puts one of their own in jeopardy.

* * *

Gina Rappaport pulls into her driveway after a day of shopping at the exclusive International Mall. She's steeling herself for the lecture she'll get from her husband when he gets home. "I work my fingers to the bone," Jack will say, glaring at her and waving his arms, "and all you know how to do is shop!" But what's the benefit of being married to that rich son-of-a-bitch if she can't spend his money. She was eighteen years old, the second runner up in the county's Miss Citrus pageant, where she met one of the judges, Jack Rappaport, a man almost twice her age. When they married, her friends said that all he wanted from her was sex. So what? All she wanted was to get out of the trailer park and into Jack's four-bedroom house. He gets his sex and she's enjoying the perks of being married to a rich guy.

As Gina enters her driveway, she doesn't notice the car parked across the street. She turns off the engine of her Lexus, opens the car door, slides out of the driver's seat, and takes a deep breath, her last.

* * *

"So, you're a big shot now," Tony jokes, as we walk into the Sheriff Department's Technology Center for the semester's first *Tech Squad* workshop. "Community Association Board of Directors. I'm impressed with your overwhelming victory."

"I won by five votes."

"Will you be sworn in at this Wednesday's board meeting?"

"I will, but there's no formal swearing-in ceremony. I think the board president just welcomes me."

"Well, I'll be there. I've been invited to talk about the recent burglaries in Sun Coast Shores. I'll also be making a presentation at next week's community meeting."

* * *

"Hey, Doc," Diego motions to the snack table. "Last semester, Alex told us about the farmers market where he works on weekends. All of us went last Sunday and bought these fresh fruits for today's meeting. We got strawberries, blueberries, mangos, papayas, apples, and this one," he says, pointing to a bowl at the end of the table, "whose name I don't remember."

"Lychees," Alex replies.

"Yeah, lychees. Anyway, they're real good. Try one."

86

I bite into a lychee and I'm waiting for the question I know is coming.

"We got a case today?" This time it's Judy who speaks up.

"We do."

"Is it a murder?"

"It is. Sheriff, please explain."

"You may have read in the newspaper," Tony begins, and then appears to remember the students' reaction the last time he said this, "or seen in the news feeds on your phones, about the shooting death of Gina Rappaport in Riverview last week. Two neighbors called 911 at about 6:15 in the evening, saying they heard a shot. When my officers arrived, we found Mrs. Rappaport lying in a pool of blood next to the open driver's side door. She appears to have been shot as she was getting out of her car."

"What have you learned so far?" Alex asks.

"The bullet came from a .38 caliber handgun. There are no fingerprints on the casing."

"Do you know where the shooter may have been when he fired the shot?" James inquires.

"We think he may have been standing behind a bush in front of the house. The shot entered Mrs. Rappaport's head just above her left ear. Assuming she got out of her car and was facing forward, the bush was his only hiding place. There was no gunshot residue on her head or clothing, which would indicate the shot was not fired at close range."

"Unless she knew him," Kayla says, "then he could have been standing in the open. You said Mrs. Rappaport, so I assume she was married. Was she divorced or separated, or something?"

"According to the neighbors, she and her husband, Jack, both lived in the house. Jack has an alibi. He owns three bars in the Tampa area. At the time the neighbors heard the shot, he was receiving a delivery at one of his bars."

"Did any of the neighbors see someone leaving the scene?" Judy queries.

Tony looks at me. "Your students are really picking up on police investigation procedures." He then turns to Judy. "We questioned all of the neighbors on both sides of the street. Those who were home say they heard a loud bang. Two of them said they saw a car speed away, each giving a different description. One thought it was a dark blue or black sedan, another described a tan or yellow SUV. Two homes, one east of the Rappaport's, and one three houses to the west, have surveillance cameras pointed toward the street. The video from the one to the east picked up the car speeding away but, since it showed the side of the car, it didn't display the license plate."

"What type of car was it," Judy asks, "a dark sedan or a tan or yellow SUV?"

"Neither," Tony responds. "It was a pickup truck."

Judy shakes her head. "So much for eye witness accounts."

Tony continues. "And, oh yes, before anyone asks, we did take pictures at the scene. I'd like you guys to use that Photomesh thing and Sim something,"

"Simsoft," I reply.

"Yeah, Simsoft. Let's see what they might tell us. Our photos and videos are on our web site."

James' and Kayla's fingers move quickly over their keyboards. In less than fifteen minutes James has accessed the photos and videos on the Sheriff Department's web site and created a three-dimensional view of the crime scene. Kayla then adds simulation.

"I've created multiple views of the scene," Kayla says. "One shows the killer behind the bush and another depicts him standing in the driveway. He shoots Mrs. Rappaport and either moves to a car or walks or runs away."

"Any trace evidence at the scene?" Diego inquires.

"We found hairs and skin samples by the bush," Tony responds. "That's another reason we assume the killer hid there, waiting for the victim to arrive. Once we identify a suspect, we can match DNA with the trace evidence."

As often happens in our workshop, Adiva sits quietly, listening and taking notes. She points to a section of the Photomesh video displaying a house located where the street makes a 90 degree turn to the right. "Sheriff, did you talk with the people in this house?"

"We didn't. No one lives there. According to the neighbors, the owners moved about two months ago. The house is for sale."

"I think we should take a look at that house," Adiva says.

* * *

"Why do we have to leave so early?" Shirley Greenberg asks as she and her husband pull out of their driveway. After almost fifty years of marriage, Morris Greenberg easily senses his wife's annoyance.

"We have a lot to talk about at tonight's Property Owners Board of Directors meeting. As president of the board, I want to be there early, so I can count heads and see how many of the boys are on my side before the meeting begins. Anyway, you're a woman. You just don't understand Community Association politics."

Shirley has gotten used to her husband's patronizing attitude. "First of all, my love, you and your buddies haven't been boys since the Kennedy administration, and there are women on the board, you know, or have you forgotten that Adele Becker and I were elected last November."

Morris hasn't forgotten, even though he feels that managing a community should be a man's job. Women just aren't up to the task.

Emanuel

Morris steers his BMW into his reserved Community Center parking space. He smiles as he reads the sign, *RESERVED FOR MORRIS GREENBERG – PRESIDENT – SUN COAST SHORES PROPERTY OWNERS BOARD OF DIRECTORS*. His own parking space. Everyone can see how important he is.

* * *

I take my seat at the Director's table.

"Let's get this meeting started," Morris says, rapping his gavel on the wooden table. "We have an important item to cover. First, I want to welcome our newest director, Lionel Trevor. Glad to have you on board, Lionel."

"Thanks, Morris, glad to be here."

"Tonight, we need to talk about what we're going to do to protect our community from all of those outsiders coming in through the golf course. We've had three burglaries in the last four months and the security patrol recently chased two of those farm workers from our property. Probably illegal, you know."

"I think you're jumping to conclusions," I say. "We've been assured that the farm owners don't hire illegals."

"Yeah, and I was assured that the ring I bought Shirley was 18k gold, only to find out it was only 14k. People lie, you know."

"If I had known that our community was so close to those kinds of people I would never have bought here," the board's treasurer, Jesse Albertson, says. "Last week, Laura and I were attending a wedding back in Ohio. When we got home, we found her good jewelry gone. And we thought we had a perfect hiding place."

Morris points at Tony. "Sheriff, what can you tell us about these burglaries?"

"The thief appears to know what he's doing. All the affected homes back up on the golf course. He breaks in through the rear screen doors and then picks the lock on the sliding doors that separate the lanai or pool from the

90

The Family Jewels

living room. He's very careful. We haven't found any trace evidence, such as fingerprints or hairs, in the house, or footprints in the dirt or grass outside the screen doors. All of the burglaries have occurred when the homes' residents are out of town. We talked to the two kids the Security Patrol chased. They both have alibis for the nights of the break-ins. At this point, that's what we know."

Morris turns to Bill Grogan, who had recently replaced Steve Dombrowski as captain of the community watch program.

"Bill, what have you found out?"

"Our guys are patrolling our community's perimeter and keeping an eye on the homes near the golf course."

"The volunteers should carry guns," Jesse shouts, his voice raising in anger. "Let those SOBs know that we'll shoot on sight. I'd love to get one of those wetbacks caught in my cross-hairs."

Bill is about to respond when Morris intervenes. "That's the last thing we need. We'd be on the front page of the Tampa Bay Times if we shoot an unarmed farm worker."

"Yeah," Jesse counters, "But it'd show we ain't takin' no crap from anyone, 'specially them."

"And your arrest, would also be on the Times' front page," Tony responds. "If you see anything, call 911."

"I have a proposal I'd like to present at the next Property Owners Meeting," Morris says. "We should build an 8-foot high wall around the entire community. We'll have gates that can only be opened with pass cards. That will keep those ill—," Morris glances toward me, "—those migrant workers out."

"Do you really think that's necessary?" I ask. "We live in a retirement community, not a walled fortress."

"Of course, it's necessary," Morris replies. "It's our job as members of the Board of Directors to keep the

91

community safe. What better way than a wall to keep undesirables out?"

"And what's this wall going to cost?" Bill Grogan asks. "And how are we going to pay for it?"

"I've done some preliminary research," Morris responds, "and I'm estimating we will need an assessment of about $3,000 per home to build the wall and possibly have to increase fees at least $50 a month, for maintenance. The cost will be worth it if it keeps us safe. Now how 'bout we vote to propose this at the next Property Owners' Meeting?"

I look around. The wall's cost appears to surprise some of the board members. Jesse Albertson's earlier bravado seems to have disappeared.

"Hold on," Bill Grogan protests. "I know the people who have been victims. I've been in their homes. I value safety as much as the next guy, but I think we should look for less expensive ways to protect ourselves, like surveillance camera. I suggest we table this motion until next month's board meeting. This will give us time to talk with our neighbors and see what they think."

I know that Morris wants to get the board's approval immediately but, looking around, I sense he doesn't have the votes. I've already talked with one of the wall project's strongest supporters, Robert Sloan, who had to miss this evening's meeting. He's busy entertaining his granddaughter. I assume Robert will attend next month. Morris probably realizes that delaying the vote for a month could give him the support he needs to pass the proposal.

"Maybe it's best that we hold this until our next meeting," Morris pulls his phone from his pocket, "which will be on October 11th. It will be the first item on the agenda. This can't wait."

The other members of the board nod in agreement. "OK," Morris continues, "we'll take it up next month. But remember, our goal is to protect our community. This meeting is adjourned."

Bill Grogan pulls me aside as I'm walking toward the board room's exit. "How about a cup of coffee in the bistro?"

"Happy to Bill. What's up?"

"Do you really think this wall idea has any legs?" Bill and I take our coffee and some cookies, which the Women's Club had baked, and sit at an empty table.

"I hope not," I say. "You know how some of these guys are. They see a problem and come up with a solution that's obvious, simple, and wrong. They just don't think it through."

"I hope you're right," Bill replies. "You know it's been rough since Marge died. Her last year of treatments and chemo cost us a lot out-of-pocket. An assessment and increase in HOA fees will really strap me. I'd hate to have to move. My friends here have been really supportive. So many of them include me in social activities even though we're not a couple anymore." I see the saddened look on Bill's face.

"The Social Activities Club invited me to join and suggested I help coordinate the Labor Day events," Bill continues. "They probably did it to help keep me busy and maybe because they know that Marge had me managing our social calendar. I think she did it just to give me something to do, but it did teach me a lot about how to navigate this new social media stuff." Bill pulls out his phone, brings up his virtual keyboard, accesses an app, and shows it to me. "With Marge's help, I created a Facebook account and learned to use Twitter. But being on the Social Committee? I was a general contractor before retiring. I know tools but nothing about arranging a barbecue. Don't get me wrong, their efforts are appreciated. They're even saying I should join the community's singles group. I probably will, someday, but it's only a little over a year since Marge died. It's a bit early."

"Keep your chin up, Bill," I say. "Most of us retirees have to watch our pennies. I don't think they're going to go for a wall."

* * *

"You've been awfully quiet," Morris says, turning to his wife, as they drive home from the meeting.

"What's this bravado about accepting the increased cost of your wall?"

"Our wall."

"Your wall. You know we're just getting by as it is. I've had to cash in half of my inheritance just to pay our bills, including the payments on that BMW you had to buy. Why do we need an expensive car like that just to go out to dinner or to the movies?"

"Because everyone's impressed when we pick them up in the BMW. We've got to keep up appearances. Anyway, don't worry. I'll get the money."

"I know how you plan to get the money. It'll come out of my inheritance again."

Morris doesn't say anything.

* * *

"Alex, how many times do I have to tell you, the strawberries go in front. It attracts customers," Sophia Perez tells her son as she arranges the booth for this weekend's farmers' market. "And put down that phone. We have work to do."

"I know, Ma. Our booth doesn't open for forty-five minutes and I have an online assignment to complete for the *Tech Squad*. I'm almost done."

"OK, but make sure all of the fruits and vegetables are out before the market opens."

Alex spends the next forty-five minutes alternating his attention between setting up the booth and reading the assigned article.

"OK Ma, I'm done," Alex says, as he places his phone in his pocket, "now where do you want the strawberries?"

"In front, like I just told you."

At exactly 11:00 the market opens. Business is brisk for most of the day. When traffic at the booth slows at about 4:00, Sophia takes a break and leaves her son to handle customers.

Alex's presence attracts people to their booth. At just under six feet tall, his good looks and athletic build serve as a magnet to many of the affluent teenage girls who frequent the market. Some of these girls even buy fruit.

"I'll take these two baskets of strawberries," Tiffany Sloan hands Alex a five-dollar bill. Alex had noticed Tiffany even before she approached the booth. How could he not? She's almost as tall as he is, with silky blond hair hanging below her shoulders, huge blue eyes, tanned legs, and wearing a halter top, and cutoff denim shorts. He couldn't take his eyes off her. He watched as she bent to examine the fruit baskets and then approached to pay for the ones she's selected.

"You from around here?" Alex asks.

"No, I'm spending time with my grandparents in Sun Coast Shores. I'll be here for another week, and then it's back home and then it will be off to school."

"Where do you go to school? One of those big colleges up north?"

Tiffany smiles. She's used to boys thinking she's older than she is. "I graduated high school in June. I'm taking a few months off. I'll start at U. Mass. in January."

"Enjoy your stay," Alex says, as he turns to put the money into the cash register and get change. Tiffany spies the phone in his pocket.

"Can I see your phone?"

"Sure."

Tiffany takes Alex's phone, taps a few keys, and slips it back into his pocket. Their eyes lock for just a moment.

They both smile. The farmer's market will close at 5:00 PM. Tiffany knows she can expect a call or text, probably that evening. She's right.

* * *

It takes Alex less than thirty minutes to walk the mile and a half from the two-bedroom mobile home where Carlos, Sophia, Alex and Juan Perez live to the Sloan's four-bedroom dwelling in luxurious Sun Coast Shores. Both are in the same Hillsborough County zip code, but they could be in different universes. Alex has been in some of these homes. When he delivers produce from the farm, he enters through the wide front entrance. This time he takes a slightly longer route, through the golf course. Tiffany told him to come to the back door of the screened lanai. She says her grandparents, who are away overnight, wouldn't approve of her seeing someone like him. Their neighbors are nosey and would be sure to spot him if he drove up to the front door. *I guess I should be insulted*, he thinks, *but oh, those legs*. The sight of her walking up the path to the booth in those cut-off jeans is burned in his memory.

"Hey, Alex, come on in."

His eyes light up and his heart begins to pound. She's wearing that same outfit she wore when he met her at the farmer's market. "Are you sure your grandparents are gone for the night?"

"Yup. When they go to one of those political fund raiser parties at a fancy hotel in Tampa, Grandpa always has too much to drink. Grandma reserves a room at the hotel, and they spend the night. They won't be home 'til late tomorrow morning."

"This is some place. Your grandfolks rich or something?"

"Or something. They owned a jewelry store before they sold it and retired. In fact, that's how I can go to college. Grandpa will pay the bills as long as I behave myself."

"So, you're going to behave yourself?"

96

"Or be sure Grandpa doesn't find out. Come on, let me show you around the house."

"This is awesome," Alex exclaims, as Tiffany guides him to the master bedroom. "Your grandparents' bedroom is larger than our whole house. Their closet is bigger than the room I share with my brother."

"Here, let me show you something." Tiffany bends to pull a book from a bookshelf sitting in the corner of the large room.

"Moby Dick, I've never read it," Alex says.

"Neither have I." She hands the book to Alex. "Open it."

Alex sees a hollowed-out interior. "This is Grandma's hiding place for her good jewelry," Tiffany offers. "She showed it to me a few days ago, says it will be mine after she dies. Aren't these pieces beautiful?"

"They sure are." Alex doesn't know quite what he's looking at. His mother has no jewelry other than the small wedding band she wears. His dad always tells her he'll get her a real gold band someday.

Tiffany replaces the book and leads Alex back to the living room and motions him to the couch. He sits and she curls up right next to him. "Do you like old movies? I do."

If she had said she liked lima beans and asked him if he wanted some, he would have answered yes. Whatever she wants. "I sure do. Do you have one you want to watch?"

"Yup. Grandpa recorded one called *Casablanca*. It's something about World War II. We studied it in school. Did you?"

"I studied about World War II, but I never heard of *Casablanca*."

"OK, let's try it."

Alex had been paying so much attention to Tiffany, he hadn't noticed the huge TV mounted on the wall. It wasn't anything like that little one he had on the table in his bedroom. The young girl pushes some buttons on the remote and the screen comes to life. The movie is actually pretty good, at least what he sees of it. This evening is turning out even better than he thought it would.

The movie's final credits roll. Tiffany turns off the TV. "Come on, Alex, let me show you my room."

It's 4 o'clock in the morning when Tiffany wakes Alex. "You'd better leave now," she says, handing Alex his clothing. "This time of the year the golfers get out around six. There could be questions if one of them spots you crossing the second tee."

"You're right. Can I see you again?"

"I'm going home on Thursday, but I'll be back. Got to keep gramps happy."

* * *

Morris Greenberg spies Robert Sloan as the two men enter the Community Social Hall. "You with us on the wall issue?"

"I am," Sloan replies.

"Then we should have the votes at the next Board meeting."

* * *

"Let's get this meeting started." Morris Greenberg raps his gavel on the folding table as he faces the large group of Sun Coast Estates residents who have gathered in the social hall. Morris likes rapping his gavel. It's one of the perks of being President of the Property Owners Association. "We have a lot to cover."

I take a seat next to Bill Grogan. The Community Social Hall is packed, and people are standing along the sides of the room. Morris estimates there are twice as many residents attending this month's meeting than usually show up. He knows why. "I know that you're all concerned with the home invasions we've recently had. So, let's get right to it. I've invited Sheriff Maggio to talk to us this evening about where their investigation stands, and what we can do to protect ourselves."

Tony repeats what he told us at the board meeting, stating how the thief appears to know what he's doing, that he breaks in through the rear screen doors and then picks the lock on the sliding doors. He states that his investigation hasn't found any trace evidence, such as fingerprints, or hairs in the house, or footprints in the dirt or grass outside the screen doors. "Right now," he states, "we have very little to go on, but I'm sure we'll get a break soon."

"So, we have to live with these burglaries," Jesse Albertson protests. "Is that what you're saying?"

"Until we get a lead, yes, but there are some steps you can take to protect yourself. Ensure your alarm systems are working and that they're armed whenever you're not home. If you have a safe, be sure it's locked. Don't put your valuables in obvious places like jewelry boxes in your bedroom. That's the first place a burglar looks."

"What about in the freezer?" Jack Becker asks. "I've heard that's a good place."

"The burglars have heard that too, so that's the second place they look. No, I suggest less obvious hiding places."

"Like where?" Bill Grogan inquires.

"Like where?" Bill Grogan inquires.

"Like a hollowed-out book," Robert Sloan says.

"That's an excellent hiding place," Tony replies. "I've been in many of your homes and I know that some of you have extensive book collections. A burglar isn't going to take the time to pull out each book on the chance that he'll find something. Other good locations are empty food and cleaning materials cans, hollowed out building materials, such as window sills and floor boards and the bottom of a house plant. You can also put them in a plain box on a closet shelf labeled something like 'Christmas Decorations'. Burglars probably would just ignore a box like that. Don't make it easy for these guys to find your valuables."

Emanuel

"Thank you, sheriff," Morris says. "I'm sure you'll have this case solved quickly. Meanwhile, we'll do everything we can to protect ourselves."

* * *

A low-hanging fog hangs over the muggy summer night air as he steers his golf cart over the fairway and past the 14th hole. He hates what he's doing. The last time he threw up, he just barfed his guts out on the fairway, but he has no choice. He stops his cart between two unoccupied houses, picks up an empty plastic bag and broom he brought, slips on a pair of surgical gloves and steps onto the grass. He removes his shoes and places them, along with the broom, just outside the lanai door of the larger of the two houses. *No sense taking a chance of being identified by shoe prints*, he thinks. He strides in his stocking feet to the lanai door, pulls a screw driver from his pocket and, with a quick twist, opens the door. He crosses the lanai and pops the sliding door entrance.

The large living room is dark, except for a night light in an electric socket. He knows where to go. He's been in this house before. He crosses the plush area rug and hardwood floor and heads straight for the bedroom bookcase. The bottom shelf contains five hard back books. He pulls them out and finds one hollowed-out that contains gold rings and necklaces. The necklaces contain what appear to be inlaid emeralds. He also finds two matched sets of emerald earrings, and a diamond ring. He applies a technique called the fog test, or breath test, to determine if the diamond is real. Genuine diamonds are efficient heat conductors. When you breathe on them, the fog disperses immediately. It's genuine. The inside of the gold necklaces are stamped *18k*. He has no way to test the emeralds but guesses that, since they're in this book, they're valuable. He places the jewelry in the bag he's brought and returns the books to the shelf. As he leaves the bedroom and enters the living room, he spots the display case abutting both sides of the TV. He grabs

100

the Waterford Crystal and Hummel figures, places them gently in the bag and leaves the house the same way he had entered. He exits the lanai, slips into his shoes and uses the broom to ruffle the grass, erasing any footprints between the cart and screen door, gets in the golf cart, and drives off.

* * *

"Robert, come here!" Grace Sloan shouts.

"I'll be there in a minute. I'm getting the luggage out of the car."

"Come now. We've been robbed!"

Robert Sloan drops the suitcases he's holding and runs to his wife. As he enters the bedroom, he sees her anguished face.

Grace stands next to the bookcase in tears, holding the empty hollowed out book. "They got the good stuff we kept when we sold the business, along with the Hummel figures and Waterford crystal dish. We go to visit my sister in Fort Lauderdale for a weekend and this is what happens!" They both realize how much had been taken.

Robert Sloan is a distinguished looking gentleman. At age 70, he's maintained his athletic build and a full head of black hair, graying at the temples. Only Grace knows that he has been dyeing it for over 25 years.

The women in the Sun Coast Shores Women's Club always admire Grace's jewelry and Grace enjoys showing it off. Now it's gone.

"It's OK," Robert says. "We're fully insured. I'll contact our agent."

"That's not the point," Grace shouts, tears rolling down her face. "I won't be able to replace that jewelry. Thank God Tiffany went home last week. I would never forgive myself if she had been hurt."

"Well, she wasn't here. Now try to calm down." Robert knows he must stay calm and focused even though he's shaking at the thought of his home being invaded.

Emanuel

Sheriff Tony Maggio and Deputy Daniel Boudreau arrive within thirty minutes of Robert's call. The sheriff speaks with the Sloans and prepares his burglary report while the deputy takes pictures of the crime scene, dusts for fingerprints, and collects trace samples that might identify the thief.

The deputy grabs a small box he's carrying. "Mr. and Mrs. Sloan, can we get your fingerprints?"

"Sure."

The deputy places all ten fingers of both Sloan's hands on the box's glass. "I found four distinct fingerprints on the hollowed-out book. I'm assuming yours will be on it. We'll compare the prints I found to yours, which should eliminate two of the four. Any idea who the other two may be?"

"I showed the jewelry to our granddaughter, Tiffany, when she was visiting. I wanted her to see what she will inherit. She's home now in Baker's Crossing."

"We'll ask the Bakers Crossing police to get her prints."

The sheriff could see the anger in Grace's eyes. "You're saying Tiffany might have taken the jewelry! Absurd! She'll inherit it when I'm gone"

"Would anyone else have touched the book?"

"No one."

The deputy turns to the sheriff. "It looks like the burglar may have gotten sloppy. I'm assuming two of the fingerprints are the Sloans' and one is probably Tiffany's. The fourth could be the thief's."

* * *

"Screw you," the man mumbles, as the black Buick speeds past and the driver gives him the finger. It's 2 o'clock in the morning. He has just exited I-75 onto I-10 going west, toward his Alabama destination. He makes sure he drives just below the speed limit. He even pulls over when he texts Skip that he is on his way. He can't get stopped by the cops. His mind's racing.

The Family Jewels

The man's thoughts turn to the leather satchel in his car's trunk. *How stupid are these people in Sun Coast Shores? They install double locks on their front doors. They forget about the screen door to the lanai and the sliding glass doors to their living room. They're easy pickins'. All I have to do is find their good jewelry and get out. They're not happy when they get home, but I don't care.*

He turns north on Route 231 and veers left on to the dirt road just south of Dothan, across the Florida Alabama border. He meets the rough looking man he knows only as Skip. He guesses his fence to be somewhere in his early 50s, but it's hard to tell. Skip's weathered and scarred face tells him much about the life the man has led but little about his age.

"Let's see what you've got," Skip rummages through the satchel he takes from the man's trunk. "I'll give you $5,000."

"What! You'll get four times that when you sell it."

"Take it or leave it," Skip says, handing over a roll of bills.

"I guess I have no choice. Don't get lazy and try to sell it all in one place. We don't want to call attention to ourselves."

"You think I'm stupid?" Skip replies. His gravelly voice sounding menacing. "This stuff'll be scattered over ten states."

The man pockets the cash and heads back to Florida. He knows that Skip will make a pretty penny on this haul, but he also knows his fence will be here in a few weeks when he needs him again.

* * *

Dean Donna Mangano and I are in the Tech Center a half hour before our workshop is to begin. The Dean had asked if she could observe my class. I welcomed her but said there was a price. The dean's family owns Manganos,

103

Emanuel

a renowned Italian bakery in Brandon. I told her about our snack table. She didn't hesitate to offer to provide guava cheese turnovers, cinnamon sticks, and cannolis. She also arranged for Italian subs with prosciutto.

I spot Tony as he opens the door to the lab. He gestures to me to join him in the hallway, a grim look on his face.

"What's up, Tony? Something wrong?"

"I'm afraid I have some bad news. We've had to arrest one of your students, Alex Perez."

"Why?" I try to keep my voice down so the others in the workshop don't hear.

"We believe he's behind those Sun Coast Shores burglaries."

"Impossible!"

"Let's talk in your office after the workshop. I'll fill you in."

Tony and I enter the lab. I try not to show my concern to the class. I'll have to wait until after today's session to find out what happened.

I stand at the front of the class and gesture to Adiva. "At our last meeting, you asked the sheriff to check a third neighbor's house. I understand that helped solve Mrs. Rappaport's murder. Tell us what you found."

"Shouldn't we wait for Alex? He never misses our workshop."

I glance at Tony. "No, I'll check on him if he doesn't come."

"OK, Doc. I've asked James and Kayla to run the Photomesh video and Simsoft simulation. At our last workshop I noticed a house at the point where the street turns to the right. I thought I saw a surveillance camera above the garage. I enlarged the photo. I was right. When the sheriff interviewed the owners, they said they need to monitor the house until it is sold. The camera's storage has video from the date and time of the murder. As you can see, the truck that one of the neighbor's surveillance cameras spotted turns right where the street curves. After the turn we are able to see the license plate." Adiva points to the screen. "Photo enhancement gives a clear picture of the plate. Motor vehicle records identify the truck's owner as Benny Phillips, a man with an extensive police record."

"A rap sheet as long as his arm," Diego smiles and turns to face the others. "Do I have the jargon right, Sheriff? I think that's what they call police records on all the cop shows I watch."

"You got it right," Tony says.

"At this point," Adiva continues, "I'll ask the Sheriff to take up the story."

"Thanks, Adiva. We picked the guy up. He denied everything, but we matched his DNA with the trace evidence we found near the bush where he hid. A search of the Florida Department of Agriculture's records shows he has a concealed carry permit."

Judy has a puzzled look on her face. "Department of Agriculture?"

"Yup," Tony replies. "In Florida, that's who issues these permits."

"Have you found the gun?"

"We have. Adiva, please tell them how."

"Mr. Phillips' truck has a GPS system, which tracked its route after the murder. About ten minutes after he left Mrs. Rappaport's house, he stopped by a wooded area for approximately three minutes."

"I didn't know a GPS tracker records the time a car is traveling," Kayla says.

"Some do and some don't," Adiva replies. "His does."

Tony picks up the story. "We guessed that he got out of the car, walked a few feet into the woods, and tossed the gun. We were right. We found it in a clump of trees. A ballistics test verified that the bullet that killed Mrs. Rappaport came from his gun. Phillips knew we had him cold, but he insisted on a plea deal before he told us who

Emanuel

hired him. Once the deal was in place, he fingered the husband and said he was paid in cash. We picked up Mr. Rappaport, who denies everything. We checked Rappaport's bank statements, searching for a large withdrawal he would need to pay Phillips."

"Did you find anything?" Judy asks.

"Nothing," Tony responds. "Bar patrons often pay in cash, so it would be easy for Rappaport to use money from the business to pay Phillips. The only evidence we had was Phillips' statement. DAs don't like to try cases that hinge on the testimony of a single co-conspirator, especially one with a rap sheet as long as his arm." Tony glances toward Diego and smiles. "Defense attorneys know this. We had to get something else. This is where technology helped us again. Adiva, please finish the story."

"Everyone take out your phones," Adiva instructs. "If you look at your text messages and email folders, you'll see that everything is saved. Both the husband and Phillips used burner phones, but we got lucky. Our suspect hadn't thrown his away. He explained to the sheriff that Rappaport paid him half of what he was owed when he agreed to kill his wife and would pay the other half after the job was done. When we arrested him, he had not yet received the second installment. He needed the phone to contact Rappaport to arrange to get his money."

"Have you found Mr. Rappaport's burner?" Diego asks.

"We haven't," Tony responds, "but we located the store where they were sold from the serial number on Phillip's phone. The store's owner found the exact date and time they were purchased. A video camera clearly shows Rappaport buying two burners. We were able to track calls and text messages between Phillips and Rappaport. It's going to be hard for a defense attorney to convince a jury that the killer was not communicating with the man who hired him. We also found texts from the husband to a girlfriend and, guess what, the girlfriend's Facebook page tells the entire story of their relationship, including Rappaport's promise to marry her and take a long trip after he *cleared up some loose ends*. The girlfriend cooperated fully, since she had committed no crime and, as she said, 'A man who kills his wife to marry his girlfriend, will kill his new wife to marry his next girlfriend'."

"Thank you, team, and thank you Sheriff."

* * *

Tony follows me to my office. "Can you tell me what's going on? Why do you think Alex is involved with those burglaries?"

"We know that the thief gained access to the homes that were robbed through the screened lanai and sliding glass doors. We checked for fingerprints."

"Did you find Alex's prints?"

"We did. They were all over the Sloan's home."

"Did Alex explain how they got there?"

"He says the Sloan's granddaughter, Tiffany, invited him over one evening when her grandparents were away."

"Then, that explains his prints in their home."

"In the living room, yes, and, if you believe Alex's story, in Tiffany's bedroom, but his prints were also all over the Sloan's bedroom, and on the hollowed-out book where Mrs. Sloan kept her jewelry."

"How does Alex explain this?"

"He insists that Tiffany gave him a tour of the house, so his prints would be in every room, and that she showed him the jewelry. He admits that he touched the book."

"Have you asked Tiffany?"

"Not yet, she was only visiting for a short while. She's back home in Bakers Crossing, Massachusetts. We've asked the police there to talk with her."

"Were Alex's fingerprints in the other homes?"

Emanuel

"No, but he could have worn gloves."

"It seems odd that he would have worn gloves for the earlier burglaries but not at the Sloan's."

"I can't explain that, but even if we can't get him for the other burglaries, we got him for the Sloan's."

"Can I talk with him?"

"Sure. Follow me to the station?"

* * *

When we enter the precinct, I see Carlos and Sophia Perez sitting on a bench in the waiting area.

"Professor Trevor, you've got to help us." Sophia springs from the bench where she and her husband are sitting. Fear is in her eyes. "They say my Alex stole some stuff. He couldn't have. He would never do that. You know him. He wants to be a policeman. He would never steal anything."

I put my arm over Sophia's shoulder. "Mrs. Perez, do you have a lawyer?"

Sophia begins to cry. "They assigned a lawyer to us through something called, I think, a public defender. He's with Alex now. But I don't know. That lawyer seems so young."

"Let me talk with Alex." The three of us enter the Interrogation Room where Alex, and a man who looks no older than my students, are sitting at a table. I introduce myself to the lawyer who gives me his business card and tells me his name is Peter Martinez. I then turn toward Alex. "Can you tell me what happened?"

"Like I told the cops, I was at Tiffany's house. She invited me, and we watched TV." I had a feeling they had done more than watch TV. "I didn't steal any jewelry. You'll see when the cops talk with Tiffany."

"I told you not to fool around with those girls," Sophia scolds. "They only cause us trouble."

Carlos, Sophia, Alex, the attorney, and I all look up when Tony enters the room. "The Bakers Crossing police just got back to us."

"See, I told you," Alex declares. "I was with her when her grandparents were gone. Can we go home now?"

"I'm sorry, you can't," Tony responds. "Tiffany Sloan says she doesn't know you."

"But that can't be." Alex sits up straight in his chair. "Why would she say that? We spent the evening at her house. I can show you. She put her number in my phone and we texted. Sheriff, you confiscated my phone. If I can see it, I will show you." Tony leaves the interrogation room and returns a few minutes later with Alex's phone. Alex presses a few buttons. "I don't understand. Her phone number and texts are gone. That can't be."

"I'm sorry." Tony places his hand on Alex's shoulder. "There's nothing showing that you were with Tiffany. We'll have to hold you."

Tony leaves the interrogation room and heads to his office. I follow him. "What's going to happen now?" I ask.

"The DA plans to charge him and his lawyer will probably recommend that he take a plea. I feel bad for the kid but there's nothing I can do."

I return to my office and try to get work done, but I can't get my mind off Alex. There must be something I can do. I look up and see Judy walking in the hallway. As usual, she's glancing down at her phone. I sit up bolt straight in my chair, take my own phone out of my pocket, and press a few buttons.

"Tony, we're going to need some of your subpoenas."

* * *

"If we want to build a wall, we're going to have a $3,000 assessment and increase the monthly fees by at least $50," Bill Grogan says. "Morris Greenberg and his crowd don't seem to care about cost, but I do, and I think the rest of you do too or you wouldn't be here."

Twenty-three Sun Coast Shores residents opposed to building the wall are meeting in Bill Grogan's living room

Emanuel

having agreed they will attend the next board meeting to oppose its construction.

"You're right," Dave Shuster responds. "We don't want to live in a walled fortress. I spent my life living in open communities and, yes, we did have some crime. We let the police handle it. There's no reason to become a group of scared rabbits and panic because there might be some bad guys among us."

"I understand where the pro-wall group is coming from," Jesse Albertson declares. "When I moved here, I didn't realize we'd be so near all of those migrant workers. I should have checked it out first. But, still, a $3,000 assessment and a $50 a month increase. I just can't afford it."

Another resident is about to comment when the doorbell rings.

"Oh, good evening sheriff," Bill says, as he answers the door. "Can I help you?"

"Are you Bill Grogan?" the sheriff asks.

"Yes."

"Please turn around, Mr. Grogan. You're under arrest."

"For what!"

"For grand larceny."

The other residents stare in disbelief as the sheriff reads Bill his rights.

* * *

The students are finishing the pre-class snacks Judy's provided. "This, what do you call it, Kugel, is delicious," Diego announces. "I bet it would taste even better with some of my Aunt Isabella's salsa on it."

"Don't even think about it," Judy snaps, gently punching Diego on his arm.

The entire class breaks into loud applause when Alex enters the room.

"Welcome back, Alex, or should we say, almost convict 35842," James teases.

The Family Jewels

"That's not funny. But I do want to thank Doc, here. I understand he's the one who solved the case."

"I did, and today we're going to talk about it. I glanced out my office window the other day and noticed one of my students walking down the hallway, totally engrossed in her phone." Everyone looks at Judy. "That's when it hit me. We had missed a key point. Every one of the burglaries occurred when the people in the house would be away for at least two or three days. How did the burglar know when people would be traveling? Can anyone guess?" Alex's hand shoots up. "No fair, Alex, you already know. Anyone else?"

"Social media," Judy says. "We all put our comings and goings on social media. All of my friends know my social calendar."

"Exactly. That's how Bill Grogan knew when the Sloans and the others would be out of town. The sheriff got warrants to view the social media of all the victims. Bill was the only one who accessed all their accounts.

"After a recent board meeting Bill told me that his wife had given him the responsibility for managing their calendar. That, and his work on the community Social Activities Committee, meant that he had friended a large chunk of our neighbors on Facebook, including those who were robbed. He was able to find out when people would be away."

"You mean that even you old—," Adiva hesitates, "—I mean retired people, use social media?"

"We sure do," I reply.

"I can attest to that," Judy chimes in. "Remember, when we were discussing the murder at our local theater, I told you how my grandpa reads his newspaper every day. Well, last July, he finally bought a smart phone. He now subscribes to three newspapers and schedules his bridge games and golf tee times on it. At our weekly family dinners, grandma often has to remind him to turn it off."

111

Emanuel

"Sounds familiar," Kayla says.

"But why did Mr. Grogan do it," James inquires.

"After one of our community meetings," I reply, "Bill told me how his wife's illness before she died depleted their savings. He needed the money."

"But how did he know who had valuable jewelry?" Kayla asks.

"Many of my neighbors like to show off," I reply. "At social events, those who have expensive jewelry often flash it around and tell everyone how fortunate they are to be able to afford it."

"I guess that's important to them," Judy comments. "I hope I never get that way."

"Bill paid very close attention at these events," I continue. "He knew who owned expensive jewelry. All he had to do was wait until one of those people would be out of town. In his capacity as head of the Security Squad, no one questioned his riding in his cart across the golf course late at night."

"But how did Mr. Grogan know to look in the hollowed-out book?" Diego asks.

"The sheriff made a presentation to our community association, explaining how we can protect ourselves against burglary. Robert Sloan suggested we could hide valuables in a hollowed-out book. Bill Grogan was at that meeting and I'm sure he took note of Robert's comment.

"The final nail in Bill's coffin was on his phone. There were multiple calls to a fence in Alabama. He didn't even have the sense to use a burner. When the Houston County, Alabama sheriff's deputies arrested the fence, he still had some of the stolen jewelry in his possession."

"So, Alex's fingerprints in the Sloan's house got there the way he says they did," Adiva offers. "Why does Tiffany deny it?"

"I think I know," Alex replies. "Her grandparents are going to be paying for her education as long as she behaves herself. I guess she figures our evening together wouldn't count as behaving herself. Her free ride to college is more important to her then keeping me out of jail."

"But Alex insists he had text messages and phone calls to and from Tiffany," one of Tony's deputies notes. "We didn't find anything on Alex's phone and the Baker's Crossing police didn't find calls or messages on Tiffany's."

"Does anyone want to fill the deputy in?" I ask.

"When you delete something from a phone, it's not actually deleted, it's just covered up," Alex responds.

Tony explains further. "Our warrants included permission to access Tiffany's and Alex's phones and social media accounts. She had erased all evidence of her communications with Alex from their phones. We were able to retrieve it. It confirmed everything Alex told us."

"But, how did she get to your phone?" Judy asks. "Never mind, I think I can guess."

Alex appears embarrassed. "I must have fallen asleep."

"You men are all alike."

"I bet you're glad that's over," James says.

"I wish I never met Tiffany." *But oh, those legs...*

Emanuel

SOUTHERN FRIED MURDER

The Tech Squad is riding high. The Tampa Bay Herald featured us in its Sunday Education section, showing how we helped convict three murderers and a thief while exonerating one of our own. WTAM TV did a segment on our exploits. Prior to the TV interview, I asked the class to turn their phones off. The taping took two hours and I could see Judy was having difficulty not looking at her screen for that length of time. As soon as the cameras stopped rolling, she pulled out her phone.

Our next case had a disturbing effect on James. In fact, if it wasn't for his persistence it might not have become a case at all. Let me explain.

* * *

"Ladies and gentlemen," Beatrice Forsyth says, standing behind a podium in the Sun Coast Shores all-purpose room, "let's settle down. We have a lot to cover this evening."

"She's in full *Gone with the Wind* mode tonight," Jenny DuBois, sitting in one of the folding chairs placed in a semi-circle in front of Beatrice's podium, whispers to Carole Stapleton. "And that drawl; Scarlett O'Hara would be proud."

"Is her drawl really that pronounced?" Carole asks. "I was raised in Alabama, just like she was. My family's accent isn't nearly that heavy."

"Either is hers. I was behind her at the supermarket last week. She didn't know I was there. She was yelling at that hunk of a husband of hers and she sounded like the rest of us."

Emanuel

The South Coast Shores community formed clubs based on the residents' interests. Many organized around the areas of the country where they spent most of their lives. There's a group of New Englanders, New Yorkers, and Chicagoans. Beatrice, Jenny, and Carole, along with approximately forty other men and women, formed the Southern Heritage Club, to honor their regional roots.

"This evening we'll be discussing our activities for Southern Heritage Day," Beatrice continues, "which we'll be celebrating in just five weeks."

"Is that really a recognized holiday?" Carole inquires.

"It is, sort of," Beatrice replies. "In Alabama and Mississippi there's a holiday called Confederate Memorial Day. All state employees have the day off, and many businesses do the same. My daddy always closed his store to honor the Confederate dead. With all the Yankees here at Sun Coast Shores, we had to give it another name but, what the heck, if the New England Club can throw a beer party every August 3, Tom Brady's birthday, we can have our Southern Heritage Day."

Annabelle Tragg, most recently of Baton Rouge, raises her hand.

"Yes," Beatrice motions to Annabelle.

"I'm new here. This is my first meeting. What do we do on Southern Heritage Day?"

"I'm glad you asked. That's what we'll be talking about this evening." Beatrice motions to Jenny to join her at the podium. "Jenny's our program chairman and the person responsible for planning our celebration."

"Thanks, Bea." Beatrice glares at Jenny and Jenny knows why. Beatrice demands that everyone call her Beatrice, not Bea. Jenny likes to call her Bea, just to annoy her. "We begin the day with a golf cart parade around the community. Let me show you our slides from last year." Jenny fumbles with the computer, obviously having difficulty displaying the PowerPoint presentation. "I just don't understand this technical stuff," she flutters,

116

as error messages flash on the screen. "I must be so dumb."

"Here, let me help you," Harrison Forsyth, Beatrice's husband, says, as he reaches the podium and takes the mouse from Jenny. Harrison likes to come to people's aid whenever he can. Most of the women in the club are pretty sure that Jenny doesn't need assistance, but she knows, if she acts the damsel in distress, Harrison will come to the rescue.

Beatrice glares at Harrison as he walks from the podium and returns to the seat next to her.

"Thanks, Harrison," Jenny says. "As you can see, last year's theme was the antebellum south." She displays the slides, showing residents in costume, Harrison as Rhett Butler. The women all agree that Rhett was a perfect costume for the dashing Harrison. Jenny pauses the slides for a moment when Harrison and Beatrice appear on the screen. Harrison looks splendid as Rhett, and Beatrice, all 220 pounds of her, trying to look like Scarlett.

"Tell them about this year's theme," a male voice from the back of the room shouts.

"I'm getting there, Jerry. This year, a few of our members suggested we do something more in tune with the male interest, and what do southern men think about more than anything else—," Jenny pauses for a moment, letting everyone wonder what's coming next, "—college football."

"Go, Hilltoppers," Jerry shouts. "That's the University of Kentucky—y'all."

"Those of us who went to college," Jenny continues, "know that bowl games are as much a part of our heritage as warm summer breezes. So, this year, our golf cart parade will celebrate our great college football heritage. Anyone who didn't attend college can adopt one of our teams. And those who got your education up north, or out west, we'll let you join the festivities once you admit your mistake and grovel."

"And what happens after the parade?" Annabelle asks.

"That's when we eat. We'll have a tailgate party, but with a little southern flare. Carole is in charge of the food. Can you tell us what's on the menu?"

Carole steps to the podium. "We'll have the usual, hot dogs, hamburgers, baked beans, coleslaw, potato salad and, of course, beer."

"Of course," two of the men say, simultaneously.

"But we'll add a little southern flare. Our friend, Drew Delacroix," she points to a gentleman in the third row, "has agreed to add some Cajun delicacies."

Drew, a retired chef from one of the most prestigious restaurants in New Orleans, stands. "They'll be hush puppies, apple fritters, jambalaya, craw fish pie, filet gumbo, and, my specialty, mint julep. I found a place online to buy the mint, and the super fine sugar we need, and Jerry, back there, has agreed to supply the bourbon."

"Kentucky bourbon," Jerry says.

"Is there any other kind?" Drew responds.

"No."

"So, get your golf carts decorated and dig out your old school jerseys," Jenny continues, "and don't forget to try them on before the big day. If these are the jerseys you wore back in college, they might be a little snug."

The meeting breaks up and everyone heads toward their cars or carts.

Beatrice glares at Harrison from the passenger seat as he drives home. "I saw you flirting with Jenny on the podium. *'I just don't understand this technical stuff,'* she says, mocking Jenny. *'I must be so dumb.'* Then, of course, you ran to her rescue."

"What did you expect me to do, leave her up there, floundering?"

"You could have helped her, but you didn't have to put your hand over hers on the mouse. And that look she gave you, I know what that means."

Harrison is used to Beatrice's jealousy any time one of the women in the community pays attention to him. There are times he would like to return the attention, but he knows the price. Their money is her money, from her family, and her first husband. When he met Beatrice, twenty years ago, he had all of twenty-five hundred dollars in the bank and two bookies chasing him. She paid off the bookies but let him know their deal. He would be her arm candy, living on an allowance she provided, and he would obey her rules, one of which was to not even appear to be interested in other women. Two years earlier, when he began to collect Social Security, she had reduced the allowance by the amount of the monthly check. Before he met Beatrice, he led a great life, but was always broke. He doesn't know what would have happened if she hadn't paid off those bookies. Now, he's just bored. He often wonders if it's worth it. He loves her money. He tolerates her. Divorce is out of the question. Their prenup would leave him with next to nothing.

"I know, dear," Harrison replies, sheepishly, as he pulls into their driveway. "I'll be careful when around these women."

"Yes, you will."

* * *

"Wow!" Judy says. "These are delicious. I never knew strawberries could be so sweet."

"That's because you never tasted strawberries fresh from the farm," Alex replies, "compliments of Mr. Granderson — and my mom."

The Tech Squad's snack table is spread with more calories than had ever been gathered in one place in all human history, strawberries and cream, strawberry shortcake, strawberry banana pudding, strawberry cheesecake and, the pièce de résistance, chocolate covered strawberries.

"I guess my diet will start tomorrow," Judy offers.

The door to the Technology Lab opens and Diego bounces in. "Did you guys see us on TV?" he asks. "We're the greatest." Kayla rolls her eyes, knowing that Diego is about to start mimicking Mohammed Ali. "We're the greatest students of all time, and we're so pretty! The students at the other colleges, they're ugly, but we're pretty." Diego goes into boxing moves. "Float like a butterfly, sting like a bee, the Tech Squad crew solves a mystery."

I'm glad to see my team in such good spirits as they take their seats at the lab's computer terminals.

"We got a case today, Doc?" Alex asks.

"Sorry Alex, we don't. Today I've invited two guests to talk about DNA testing and white hat hacking. I'm also going to show you how to use age progression software.

"James, why don't you introduce our first guest?"

"Thanks, Doc." James motions to a man, sitting in the back of the room. "This is Mr. Reynolds. He teaches music at Riverview High School. He was my favorite teacher."

"Did you pass his course?" Adiva asks. "I've heard you sing, or at least try to sing. It wasn't pretty."

William Reynolds approaches the front of the room, holding a handkerchief to his mouth. "You'll have to excuse my voice," he says. "I seem to have developed a sore throat but, yes, James took two classes with me and he did very well, not as a singer, as the young lady so aptly points out, but writing music."

"You write music?" Adiva asks, glancing toward James.

"He does," William replies. "He wrote the words and music for our school song, and three shows the Drama Club performed." He pauses, places his handkerchief over his mouth, and coughs. "Even as a freshman," he

120

continues in a raspy voice, "James always showed interest in both music and computers."

"Do you still write?" Judy asks.

"I do. Do you want me to sing a song I composed last week?"

"I think we should pass on that," Adiva chides.

"I think that's best," William responds. "It was after one of my classes, James and I were talking about computers and how they might apply to my interest in DNA analysis, which is what we're going to talk about today. Does anyone know what DNA is?" James' hand shoots into the air. "I know you do, James, anyone else?"

"I think it has something to do with looking at your cells to see who you are," Diego replies.

"That's a very good definition," William responds. "Here, let me show you a slide presentation which, I think, will help you understand a little more about it."

As usual, my students jump in with questions as William proceeds.

"How does DNA help the cops, eh— police, catch the bad guys?" Kayla asks.

"Cops is fine, Kayla," Tony replies. "DNA testing allows us to match DNA left at a crime scene with that of a suspect."

"So, DNA can show that someone is guilty?" Adiva asks.

"Not only can it confirm guilt or innocence," Tony says, "it can also point the police to other suspects. For example, DNA markers help identify ethnicity. This can lead to potential suspects or eliminate some.

"It can also point to a person's blood relative. Your DNA is not exactly the same as your siblings' or parents', but it is similar. We recently had a case where a robbery victim identified a suspect who had an alibi. We compared his DNA with trace evidence we found at the crime scene and determined that we had the wrong guy. His brother had held up the woman."

"I'm going to get my DNA tested with one of those sites we see on TV," James says. "My dad tells everyone who will listen that we're direct descendants of the Ming Dynasty. I'd love to find out. Can we compare our DNA with someone whose been dead a long time?"

"Some historical societies," William responds, "have analyzed DNA from people long deceased."

"How do they do that?" James asks.

"They can dig up bones or use clothing or other items people came in contact with, such as weapons or pottery, which they might find in a museum. So, young man, once you have your DNA, and that of a Ming Dynasty ruler, you can compare them to find out if your father's right."

James looks over at Diego and smiles. "Maybe we'll find out I'm the greatest."

"What triggered your interest in DNA analysis, Mr. Reynolds?" Alex asks.

"I want to find my father."

"You don't know who your father is?"

I can see, from the look on James' face, that he's uncomfortable with Alex's question. William notices it, too.

"It's OK, James," William says. "I'm open about it. I was born after my mother was raped."

"And he wasn't caught?" Alex responds.

"No, he wasn't. My mother didn't see his face and she couldn't tell the Philadelphia cops much about him, except that he was big. Thirty-five years ago, a black woman's rape was not a high priority, and there was very little police investigation. I've seen the incident file. There's not much in it. I'm hoping that DNA can help me."

"What have you learned?" Alex asks.

"Not much, so far. I'm assuming he's white. As you can see, I have a light brown complexion. My mother and her family are much darker. I've tested my own DNA, which confirms that my father is most likely Caucasian. I'm hoping, someday, to find a match. I've checked criminal databases, but no luck. I guess he must be an upstanding citizen."

My students ask a few more questions. I tell them that William has agreed to stick around after class to continue this discussion.

William takes a seat in the back of the classroom and again holds his handkerchief to his mouth.

"Take care of that cough," Judy says.

I continue. "Our next guest is a neighbor of mine in Sun Coast Shores, Dr. Harrison Forsythe. Dr. Forsythe graduated from Temple University Medical School in 1985 and spent most of his career working in the field of medical research in the Houston area. He's now retired and works ten hours a week at the local medical clinic. During the latter part of his career he became a leading expert in a field—, well, I'll let him tell you about it. They're all yours, Doctor."

As Harrison approaches the speaker's lectern, Judy's head pops up from her phone. My wife has mentioned that women in our community find Harrison quite attractive. Whenever she tells me that, I usually reply, "but not as good looking as me," at which point Deb rolls her eyes. From Judy's reaction, I guess the doctor's allure applies to women of all ages.

"Thanks, Professor. Does anyone know what a white hat hacker is?"

When someone asks a question in this workshop, I usually hear at least three or four students try to answer at the same time. This is the rare occasion when there's silence.

"I know what a hacker is," Adiva finally speaks up. "But a white hat hacker, I don't know."

"OK, what's a hacker?"

Emanuel

"Someone who breaks into a computer program, usually for malicious purposes, like to steal information or make the program not work."

"Correct. What you described is a black hat hacker. These are people who break into computers or web sites to do damage. White hat hackers are people who try to stop them and catch them when they attack."

"Like cops," Judy says.

"Just like cops."

"So, you became a white hat hacker?"

"I did. When I worked in the field of medical research, I learned about computer programming. I became adept at discovering a system's weaknesses that opened it to the black hat guys, and I created programs to thwart them. Medical organizations, such as hospitals, hired me to try to break into their networks. I reported my results and recommended ways for them to correct the flaws. Sometimes they hired me to make the corrections they needed."

"Did you ever find a program you couldn't hack?" Kayla asks.

"Never. Some were more difficult, some were easy. But I never found one that was perfectly protected."

"Why would someone want to break into a hospital's computers?" Judy asks. "Who cares what diseases someone has?"

"Has anyone ever heard of ransomware?"

"Yes," James responds, "that's where someone threatens to mess up your computer unless you pay them money."

"Exactly. Medical providers, such as hospitals and doctors, are placing an increasing amount of information online. Hackers can threaten to shut medical databases down unless they're paid. In a hospital, people can die if systems are out of service or compromised for even a few minutes."

"So, I guess, a hacker has to write a program and then figure out how to get the code into the computer to mess it up?" Alex asks.

"The second part of your statement is correct. The hacker has to find a way to get his code into the computer, and, it used to be, they also had to write it. Now, unfortunately, they can download these programs from the web. Anyone with a little computer knowledge can break into a system."

"So," Kayla says, "a bad guy could be sitting at his computer right now and destroying a hospital's system."

"He doesn't even have to be sitting at his computer. He could be off skiing if he uses a triggering mechanism."

"What's a triggering mechanism?" Adiva asks.

"A computer program that activates when an event occurs. For example, the code might be set to go live at a certain day and time, or when the hospital updates its software. The code sits dormant in the computer until the triggering event occurs. It then does its dirty work, like disabling vital programs and sending a message demanding a ransom."

My students ask a few questions about black hat and white hat hacking.

"Thank you, Harrison. Doctor Forsythe has also agreed to stick around after class."

I move on to the next topic for this workshop. "Does anyone know what age progression software does?"

Alex, my Mr. Enthusiasm, is the first to respond. "It allows us to take someone's picture and see how he might look as he gets older."

"Correct."

"How does that help law enforcement?" Adiva asks.

Tony responds. "We use it to identify people involved in cold cases, such as missing persons or suspects. Let me show you." Tony displays an old photograph on the screens. "This was taken by a surveillance camera during a 1999 robbery. We've been searching for this guy ever since. Three months ago, we arrested a man for a domestic disturbance. Professor, can you help me with this age progression stuff? I'm still learning how to use it."

I open the application and age the photograph twenty years. Within about ten seconds, we see what the suspect would look like today.

"The man we had just arrested," Tony continues, "and the suspect are one in the same. We solved a cold case."

"Hey Doc," Diego asks, "can we run a picture of ourselves through this software? I'd love to see if I'll be just as hot in thirty or forty years as I am today."

"You're so vain," Judy says, throwing a wad of paper at Diego.

"We sure can," I say. "Do any of you have a picture of yourself you can load onto your computer?" As soon as I ask this question, I realize how obvious the answer is. My students pull out their phones, where they store photos of themselves, their family and friends, and some people they hardly know. These kids all keep their lives on their phones. William and two of the sheriff's deputies join in. They each load a picture, run the software, and display their older selves on one of the Tech Labs screens.

The students are enjoying this exercise when I see a puzzled look on James' face as he observes the others in the room and leans toward one of the computer screens. "Do you have a question, James?"

"N—No, sir," James replies, as he sits back in his chair.

My students never call me *sir*. I'm going to have to follow up with him later to see what's on his mind.

"Oh, my God," Judy says, placing both hands on her head. "I'll look just like my mother."

"Look at me," Diego replies. "I'm just as hot forty years from now as I am today."

"Not so fast," Kayla chides. "How about raising that hairline, greying the hair you have left, creating a few

Southern Fried Murder

facial wrinkles because of your hard lifestyle, and, after eating all that stuff from our snack table, adding forty pounds."

Diego makes the changes. "I guess you're right. I'd better enjoy my good looks while I can."

"Does this software work in reverse?" James asks. "I'd love to see what my parents and grandparents looked like when they were my age."

"Yes, it does."

"I have a picture of my mother, here." William takes a photo from his wallet. "Let's see what she looked like when I was born."

Alex scans William's mother's picture. "You said you were born 35 years ago. Is that right?"

"Yes."

Alex runs the software and an image displays showing William's mother, thirty-five years earlier.

"She has aged gracefully," Kayla says. "She hasn't changed much,"

"No, she hasn't," Harrison replies.

Throughout my demonstration, William has been holding his handkerchief and coughing. Harrison walks over to William and puts his arm around his shoulder. "That sounds like a pretty bad cough you have, son."

"I've had it for four days. I'm taking cough medicine, but it doesn't seem to help."

"Tell you what, after the workshop I'll be heading over to the clinic. Why don't you follow me, and we'll have a look?"

"Thanks, doctor. I'll meet you over there."

My students ask a few more questions and then head toward their next class. I walk with William and Harrison to the parking lot. Harrison and I watch William get into his car, immediately set his phone on a stand on the dashboard and press a few buttons.

Emanuel

"Looks like he's synced his phone to his car's audio system," Harrison says. "They all have their own music. "I guess I'm old fashioned. I just turn on the radio and listen to whatever's on."

"Me too," I reply, "but young people, today, are different than us."

"I guess."

* * *

Three people are sitting in the waiting room as Harrison and William enter the medical clinic. "Nancy," Harrison says, addressing the attractive young woman behind the reception desk, "this is my friend, William. Please register him."

"Right away, Harr—, doctor," the woman replies, pointing to the kiosk terminal while, at the same time, keeping her eyes firmly on Harrison, "if you'll sign in, it should only be a few minutes." Harrison goes through the door separating the reception and examination areas. Nancy flips her long, auburn hair over her right shoulder and gently bites her lip. Her eyes follow Harrison until he is out of sight in the examination area. After approximately ten minutes, Nancy motions to William to come through the doors leading to the examination rooms.

Harrison has changed into his white lab coat. "Let's take a look." Harrison places a tongue depressor in William's mouth. "Yup. It looks raw. It could be strep. Let me take a swab, and have it analyzed." Harrison takes two swabs from William's throat.

"I enjoyed your presentation to Professor Trevor's class today, doctor. That white hat, black hat stuff is really interesting."

"Thanks, young man. It's funny how I got into the field. When I graduated from medical school, I planned to go into practice, just like any other doctor. I saw an article about the field of medical research. I figured I'd try that for a few years. A few years turned into over thirty and

128

medical research morphed into white hat hacking. All of a sudden, it was time to retire and I realized I had never treated a patient. That's why I volunteer to work in this clinic."

Harrison approaches Nancy and hands her a swab, his hands resting on her long, slim fingers for just a moment. "Please send this to the lab." He turns his attention again to William. "I'll send you an email with the results, which should be in about three days. If necessary, I'll attach a prescription or suggest you return for further treatment."

"Thanks, doctor." William exits the clinic and heads home.

* * *

The Sun Coast Shore's Military Veteran's Club had been formed to honor those in our community who served in the armed forces. I had been in the military because, when I graduated college, I could either risk being drafted or join the National Guard. I chose the latter. I had not been happy when my unit was activated and sent to Vietnam. After I was discharged, I had no plans to join any veteran's groups. I wanted to put the army behind me and get on with my life.

When I got home, I saw how poorly Vietnam vets were treated. I understood that many civilians felt we should have never been involved in that war. To be honest, I felt that way, but to disparage the men and women who fought, that was just wrong. It was after a July 4th parade in 1977, when I saw young people throw rotting fruits and vegetables at marchers in Chicago, I decided to get involved with our local veterans' group. It's one thing to be against a war, quite another to disrespect those of us who did as we were asked to do.

"Lionel," Dave Shuster, the club's president asks, "Do you have a report on the commemorative bricks?"

The community had dedicated an area next to our main gate to honor those who served. The memorial had

129

been controversial when our Board of Directors proposed it. Many of our residents were against it, stating they wanted our community to be associated with peace, not war. The proposal passed by a small margin and the memorial was built.

We had created a section allowing residents to purchase bricks to honor family members or buddies who had been in the armed forces. I purchased one for my father, who fought in World War II. My wife bought one for her grandmother, who was an army nurse in World War I.

"We added three bricks this month and eleven so far this year. We have a request from one of our residents which is slightly different from what we have done in the past. Beatrice, would you like to tell us what you want to do?"

Beatrice Forsythe approaches the podium. "Thanks, Lionel. Almost all the bricks are dedicated to men and woman who served in World War II and Vietnam, with a few who fought in World War I. I would like to go back further." I could tell from Beatrice's voice and demeanor that she's projecting all the southern charm she could muster. "I want to purchase a brick to honor my great-great grandfather, General James Longstreet."

There's a gasp from a man in the rear of the room. "Wasn't he a Confederate general?"

"Yes, he was."

The man who made the comment stands, his face turning red and the veins in his neck seeming to almost burst through his skin. I recognize him as Drew Delacroix. "I will not allow it. Your great-great grandfather fought to keep my great-great grandfather in chains. If he had succeeded, I might never have been born or I'd be working in the fields today, rather than enjoying my retirement. Lionel, we cannot allow a confederate memorial to be placed anywhere on Sun Coast Shore's property." Drew storms out of the room, slamming the door behind him.

I turn to Dave Shuster. "I understand Drew's concern."

"Are you going to let that—that—," Beatrice pauses for a moment, appearing to be looking for just the right words, "— man prevent us from memorializing my noble ancestor?"

In her anger, Beatrice has shed her southern belle demeaner.

"Beatrice," I say, "I suggest you let the club's board discuss this further. Do you agree, Dave?"

"I do."

"Well, I never—," Beatrice storms out of the room. I don't know how many slams that door can take.

* * *

It's the morning after the Military Veteran's Club meeting. I'd just finished three sets of tennis and decide to relax with an iced tea at the Bistro, when I spot Drew. "You OK?"

"I'm fine. I guess I shouldn't let that woman get under my skin, but she's just so phony when she tries to put on all that southern charm. She's an out-and-out racist."

"I agree that her request for a brick for her Confederate General ancestor is over the top. After our meeting last night, the board discussed it. We're not going to allow it. The vote was unanimous, but, come on, Drew, aren't you being a little harsh on her?"

"Not at all. Have you seen her posts on Neighborchat about the movie?"

Neighborchat is an online bulletin board where community members have a place to vent. "Deb follows Neighborchat; I don't. What did she say?"

"The Social Committee will be showing the movie, *Loving,* you know, the one where the Supreme Court said state laws barring mixed race marriage are unconstitutional."

"We saw it when it was in the theaters a few years ago. Deb cried through most of it."

"And if it wasn't for that decision, Vivian and I could never have married—legally."

"What did Beatrice post on Neighborchat?"

"She said it was the worst decision the Court ever made, but she called it the *Commie, Hippie* court." Drew then takes his phone from his pocket and displays other posts Beatrice placed on Neighborchat and other social media which show her racism and disapproval of miscegenation. "And you should have seen her last summer, when her grandson went over to talk with my granddaughter at the pool. She did everything she could to separate them. Terri didn't understand why she couldn't talk with the young man. The younger generation never experienced what we did, thank God."

"Don't let it get to you, Drew. We're not going to change Beatrice, and you don't want your blood pressure to spike."

* * *

"And that's a wrap," the director says.

"Thanks, Chad. We appreciate your time," Cindy Davis's heart is pounding as she removes her ear piece. She has been working for WTAM-TV for four and a half years and has just completed her first on-air assignment. Granted, it was only an interview with the local school board chairman, Chad Conklin, about the shortage of substitute teachers, but it's a beginning.

"Want to go out for a drink?" Don Lombardi, her cameraman, asks. "We can celebrate your first spot."

"Can I take a rain check, Don? I've got plans." Socializing is helpful for a young reporter, but she knows Don's reputation. He only socializes with female reporters, and she really does have important plans.

"Rain check it is, and I'll hold you to it."

There's a bounce in Cindy's step, as she heads for her car. *This is just the beginning*, she thinks. She was given this opportunity because one of the regular reporters, Rhonda Carlson, is on maternity leave. Rumor has it that Rhonda wants to cut back her hours after the baby is born, so there could be opportunities for more assignments. Hey, maybe she can be the one standing on the beach during a hurricane.

Cindy heads down Gandy Boulevard and, in less than twenty minutes, she's in the parking lot behind William's apartment. She can't wait to tell him about the interview. She opens her purse, removes her key, and enters the living room. William is lying on the couch under a heavy afghan. She leans toward him. William is staring straight ahead, holding a piece of paper in his hand.

"What's wrong babe?" Cindy asks.

"This came in the mail today."

Cindy takes the letter. It's from the Board of Education.

"After this school year," William says, "they will be cutting back the Music program. My services will no longer be needed."

"I'm sure you'll find something. You're a great teacher."

"Music teacher; no one's hiring music teachers. I don't know what I'll do if I can't teach. The business community isn't clamoring to hire music majors. I know the school needs to expand the science and math programs. The kids really need that, but is a new electronic scoreboard for the football team really more important than developing an appreciation for music?"

William's phone buzzes, signaling he has an email. "It's from the doctor. Yup, I have strep. He's attached the lab report and a prescription."

"You stay here and rest." Cindy takes William's phone and prints the prescription. "I'll take it to be filled."

When she returns, she sees William on the couch, where she left him, staring at the ceiling.

* * *

Emanuel

As I enter our clubhouse Social Hall for our monthly residents' meeting, I spot Harrison. "You alone this evening? I don't see Beatrice."

"She has planning to do for the Southern Heritage Day festivities. I get one of my rare boys' night out. I was impressed when I attended your workshop. I hear one of your students is making a presentation tonight. I'm anxious to hear what he has to say."

Harrison and I take a seat in the front row.

Sun Coast Shores Community Association President, Morris Greenberg, pounds his gavel, calling the monthly resident's meeting to order. "You all know Professor Lionel Trevor, and many of you have read about his students in the newspaper or seen them on TV. Well, one of his *Tech Squad* is here this evening to talk to us about how we can use our computers, tablets, and smart phones to help solve everyday problems. Professor."

The college requires students to complete fifty hours of community service to graduate. My workshop group has chosen to show people applications they can use to simplify their lives.

"Thanks, Morris. I want to introduce James Chang. James has prepared a presentation to show you how you can use technology to help solve common problems."

"Thanks, Doc." James plugs his phone into the computer at the speaker's terminal and presses a few buttons. An image is projected onto a screen. "Has anyone been a few miles from home and wondered if you left your garage door open?" I hear many *uh huhs* from the people in the room. "Let me show you an application, called *Champion*." He touches an icon on his phone. "I live about seven miles from here. I am now communicating with my garage door and it shows it's closed." He touches a link. "It's now showing that the door is opening." James touches another icon. "I'm now closing my garage door. You'll never again worry that you left the garage door open and, if you did, you can close it. You can trigger it even if you're miles away from home.

"Now, let me show you another cool way to use technology. Have you ever parked your car outside on a typical Florida summer day and found it blistering hot when you get in?" Another round of *uh huhs* comes from the audience. "Let me show you how to solve that problem." James presses a few buttons. "You will note that the display shows my car in the parking lot. He presses a key. "I've now started the motor and turned the air conditioner up to max. When I get to the car, I'm ready to go in cool comfort."

After turning off his motor and air conditioning, James accesses one more application, describing how he can verify his car is locked and answers a few questions from my neighbors.

I'm proud of my students. I don't know if I would have been that confident when talking to a group of adults when I was twenty years old. When James finishes, I join him at the podium.

"Thanks, James. And now the bad news. All of this technology is great, but it can be hacked." I display a portion of a video I found on YouTube. "The first part of this video shows a man in his car opening his garage door, just like James did." I then show the second half of the film. "And this shows a simulation of a burglar using a hacking device to open that same garage door. Unfortunately, anything that can be controlled remotely, via apps on your phone, can be hacked."

"I saw an item on the news where someone hacked into one of those new driverless cars and caused it to crash," Jack Gilliam, one of my tennis buddies, says. "Can that happen on today's cars?"

"It's possible," I reply. "There are chips that control locks, windows, automatic parking, lane control, and

135

braking to avoid accidents functions in your car. Technology that makes our lives easier comes with risks.

"I think I'll go out and buy a horse and buggy," Jack responds.

"How do we protect ourselves?" Sandra Paulson asks.

"Hacking often requires that the intruder be able to discover your password. It's best to use passwords that are easy to remember but difficult to guess."

"Well, you better not use our anniversary, Harry," a woman remarks, looking at the man seated next to her. "You never seem to remember that." A few of the women in attendance laugh.

"A hacker can also gain access to your computer through an email attachment or link. Has anyone ever gotten a message from someone you didn't know trying to entice you to click on an embedded file?"

"Like the one I got telling me that I may have won $10,000, and that the attached document would show me how to collect the money," a man in the front row replies.

"Did you open it?"

"I didn't."

"Good, because, if you did, it might have contained a virus that would then be loaded into your computer. Never open an email attachment unless the message is from someone you know."

I spend another ten minutes talking about the importance of securing the technology we use. After answering a few questions, I turn the podium over to Morris.

"I want to thank Professor Trevor and Mr. Chang for their informative presentations. You've given us much to think about. If there are no more questions, we'll adjourn the meeting."

"Harrison, Lionel," Morris says, as we leave the meeting room, "let's stop by the bistro for a cup of coffee, my treat."

Harrison hesitates a moment. "Not tonight, guys, I've got to go. I told Beatrice I'd be home by ten."

"Why not just text her and say you'll be late?" I ask. "That's what I'm going to do. I'll tell Deb not to wait up for me."

"I can't."

"His wife seems to have a tight rein on him," I comment, after he walks away.

"He does what he's told," Morris replies. "I think it's the pre-nup. If she divorces him, he gets next to nothing."

* * *

"Thanks, Art." William pushes his chair away from the table and turns to leave the conference room. "I appreciate your help."

William feels his stomach churning. Art Peters, his school's vice-principal, had just given him his termination package. He will be paid through the summer. His benefits will continue until September 1st. Art has also given him names of people to contact in surrounding school districts for possible future employment. He has little hope. Schools all over Florida are de-emphasizing music in favor of science, technology, engineering, and math, STEM. Surrounding states are no better.

As he starts his car, he realizes he's going to have to put on his game face. His mother is visiting. He hasn't told her about his dilemma, and he doesn't plan to. Why ruin her vacation?

He opens his apartment door and immediately hears strange noises coming from the bathroom and smells something that makes him gag.

"Ma," he shouts, running to her. He's sees his mother kneeling over the toilet and vomiting. "Ma, what's wrong?"

"I don't know. I suddenly got sick to my stomach and—oh, I'm so sorry. I messed your carpet and floor. I'll clean it up."

"You'll do nothing of the sort. I'll take care of it." William leads Lydia to the couch. Over the next hour she has two more bouts of nausea and her skin becomes pasty. "Let me take you to the clinic. I went there when I had strep. The prescription the doctor gave me cleared it up."

"OK."

He helps his mother to the car and drives the three miles to the clinic. There is only one person waiting when they arrive. In less than ten minutes the door to the examination area opens. William is glad to see that Dr. Forsythe is on duty. He explains his mother's symptoms.

Dr. Forsythe looks at Lydia and hesitates for a moment. "Eh, what was that you said, William? Tell me, again, why you brought your mother here."

William tells the doctor about his mother's nausea, for the second time. Harrison spends approximately ten minutes examining Lydia. "I don't think it's anything serious, Mrs. Reynolds. There's a virus going around. I've seen eight cases like yours in the last week. Let me give you a prescription. That should clear it up."

"I'm sorry, William, I forgot to ask, how are you feeling. You're looking much better."

"I'm feeling fine. That medication you gave me worked wonders."

"I'm glad I could help."

William guides his mother back to the car. *She seems to be feeling better already,* he thinks.

"I like that doctor," Lydia says.

William stops at the pharmacy and fills the prescription. Lydia spends the next four days with William, feeling much better by the time she leaves. Entertaining his mother helps keep his mind off his problem.

* * *

It happens so fast; the driver has no time to react. It's a bright sunny day, warm for the middle of March. *There aren't many areas of the country*, he thinks, *where you run air conditioning in March.* He had just entered the Tamiami Trail bridge crossing the Alafia river. As he lifts his left arm to lower the sun visor, and holds the steering wheel with his right hand, all four of the car's windows open. The steering wheel turns slightly to the right, the same way it does when he engages the automatic parking feature. He is headed straight for the guard rail. The scene in front of him appears to move in slow motion as he hits the concrete barrier, flips up and over, bounces twice, and falls the approximately thirty feet to the river. He feels a jolt as the vehicle hits the water. His head slams against the car's roof. The water rushes in as he loses consciousness.

* * *

It's 2:00 on a Sunday afternoon as Cindy Davis pulls her car into the WTAM TV parking lot. She really doesn't want to be here, but the newsroom always needs a crew available to cover a breaking story. The junior staff is assigned the least desirable shifts. So, this Sunday afternoon she's at her desk.

She would prefer to spend time with William. He's so depressed about his job, and she knows that the possibility of him having to relocate hangs over him. For the past week they've avoided talking about the elephant in the room. Before he got his pink slip, they were planning a wedding. But now, with her career at WTAM taking off, and him possibly having to leave the Tampa Bay area, their plans are on hold.

Cindy is reviewing the tape of the interview with the School Board Chairman, the one she hopes will run this week. Segments like this are known as filler. They're not time sensitive and are aired on slow news days. Filler assignments are given to the junior reporters. She looks forward to covering more urgent stories. She's about to get her wish.

"Cindy, Don, grab your gear," their producer says. "A car's gone off the Tamiami Trail bridge into the Alafia River. The police and emergency rescue teams are on the way. We'll need this for tonight's six o'clock news." Cindy, Don Lombardi, her cameraman, and a broadcast crew pile into a WTAM van. Ten minutes after they leave the garage, Cindy's phone rings.

"Honey," her producer says. She hates when the men call her *Honey*, but it's a price you pay in this line of work. "You'll be live. We're breaking away from our programming as soon as you get on the scene. So, move your butts." *This could be my break*, she thinks.

The scene is chaotic. Northbound traffic is being re-routed. The southbound lane is backed up for miles. Vans from the other Tampa TV stations are parked on the river's banks. Cindy, Don, and their crew move onto the bridge and approach the police barricades.

Cindy is dressed in a dark blue skirt and crisp starched white blouse, open at the neck. She can feel the perspiration begin to form under her armpits. Business attire does not always play well on warm Florida spring days, but she has no choice. Her work requires a professional look.

As Cindy approaches a police officer, she unbuttons her blouse's second button, smiles, and flips her hair back. Even the most inexperienced female reporter knows that a little cleavage and some flirting helps get men to talk. "We're live here on the Tamiami Trail bridge where, less than a half hour ago, a car went over the guard rail into the river. I'm talking with," — Cindy looks at the police officer's name tag—, "Officer Billings." The officer turns toward Cindy, removes his hat, and smooths his hair. *It works every time.* "Can you tell us what is happening?"

"Our divers have submerged and are attempting to attach a cable from a crane to the vehicle, so we can hoist it out of the river."

"Do you know how many people were in the car?"

"Only the driver, who the divers pulled out through the front window, which was open." Officer Billings points to a body covered by a tarp. Don swings the camera around to get a shot. "We attempted CPR, but it was too late.

"Has he been identified?"

"Not yet. We didn't find ID on the body. Once we get the car up, we'll look for identification."

Cindy interviews other onlookers as Don follows her with his camera. One of the crew members leans over the railing, watching the spot where the crane's cable hits the water. He will alert Cindy and Don when the car is being brought to the surface.

"Cindy, Don, it's coming up."

Cindy breaks away from the woman she's interviewing. Don points the camera at the spot where the vehicle will break the water.

"It appears the Sheriff's Department is about to raise the car." Cindy's voice gets lower and more solemn. She learned this speech technique when studying broadcast journalism at the University of Florida. A reporter adjusts her tone of voice to match the story she's covering. This one requires solemnity. "Divers have descended into the river to attach hooks extending from the cable you see, onto the vehicle. The crane is raising the car, slowly. In just a few seconds we will see it emerge from the water." Don adjusts his camera's magnification so that the vehicle breaking the surface will display full screen. "I can see the car just below the surface. I can—, Oh, my God, Oh, my God!!!" Cindy's tone changes from solemn to hysterical as she breaks down, crying, dropping her microphone. One of the crew turns toward Don, moving his hand across his throat, signaling to cut the live feed.

Emanuel

* * *

"I've never eaten anything like this, Prof," Diego says, as he attempts to get his mouth around an overstuffed corned beef and chopped liver sandwich.

I'd been in a quandary when I realized it was my turn to bring snacks to the Tech Squad workshop. My Scotch-Irish ancestors and Deb's German roots didn't lend themselves to exotic, tasty cuisine. As usual, Deb came to the rescue. She realized that our gastronomic roots came, not from another country, but from a city. "These snacks, class, come directly from the Third Avenue Deli, one of New York's most famous eating spots. We have corned beef, pastrami, knishes, chopped liver—," I see a few mouth's wrinkle at that last one. I guess, if you're not from New York, chopped liver doesn't sound very appetizing. "And for your sweet tooth, there's babka and rugelach."

"Sounds like I'll be missing my classes, tomorrow," Kayla jokes, "with an upset stomach."

Judy, who may be more familiar with deli food than the rest of the class, responds. "Don't worry, if you're not feeling well, I'll bring some of my grandma's chicken soup to first period algebra."

I look around as I am about to begin class. "Has anyone seen James? I don't think he's ever missed one of our workshops."

"We were in the student lounge yesterday," Diego answers. "He saw something on TV and just ran out of the room, got in his car, and drove off. He skipped History class."

I've never known James to skip a class. If he doesn't show up, I'll check on him.

"Do we have a case today, Doc?" Kayla asks.

"Not today, guys and gals. This afternoon, the sheriff's going to talk about a key element in crime investigation. Sheriff."

142

"Thanks, professor," Tony says. "Who can tell me the three elements of any crime that the DA needs before he or she can get an indictment and take a case to a jury?"

As often happens, Alex's hand is the first one in the air. "MOM: method, opportunity and motive."

"That's correct, and today we're going to talk about one of the *Ms*, motive. Who can tell me the three most common motives for murder that we've already discussed?"

"Let's see," Kayla responds, glancing at her notes, "greed, revenge, and—"

"—to hide a secret," Alex says.

"You guys are sharp. Now, let's look at the motives from some of the cases we've already solved. Adiva, you were instrumental in the first case. What was Professor Diaz's motive?"

"She was mad at Mr. Agnew for what he did to her sister."

"And her motive was—"

"Revenge," Adiva replies. "And revenge was also Mr. Ziegler's motive because his girlfriend was killed."

"Alex, the burglaries in Sun Coast Shores, which we first thought you did, what was Mr. Grogan's motive?"

"Greed. He needed money."

Tony continues the discussion, describing other recent cases and explaining the motives.

Our workshop time is almost over when the lab door swings open, and James flies in, marching directly toward Tony. "It's not suicide, sheriff! It can't be. Mr. Reynolds would never do that."

"Calm down, James," I say. "What're you talking about?"

"Mr. Reynolds. He died Sunday when his car went over a guard rail into the river. Sheriff, your forensic people are saying he committed suicide. I know him. He would never do that."

"That's what the evidence says, young man."

"Well, we've just got to take another look at the evidence."

I can see anger and frustration in James' face. "Tell you what, class, let's quit for the day. Sheriff, can we meet in your office to discuss Reynolds' death?"

"Sure."

"I want to come!" James demands.

"No, let me handle this with the sheriff." Tony and I retreat to his office. We agree to discuss this case at our next Tech Squad workshop.

* * *

We had a good deal of food left from last week's workshop. Some of the students had taken it home.

"No offense, Doc," Alex offers, "some of that stuff was real good, but the chopped liver— my mom says that, if we ever visit New York, we'll take our own food."

"OK class, let's settle down. This week we're going to talk about Mr. Reynolds' death. Sheriff, can you show us the evidence that points to suicide?"

"He didn't commit suicide. I know it!" I can see that James is agitated.

Tony displays a video on the screen. "This was taken from a surveillance camera mounted on the Alafia bridge. You see Reynolds' car on the entrance ramp. Note that his windows are closed. When it gets to this spot on the bridge," he says, pointing to the car, "the windows roll down. We determined that the air conditioning was on. There'd be no reason to have the air conditioning running and the windows open. At this point the car turns suddenly, and heads toward the water. As you can see, there was little traffic on the bridge, and he wasn't swerving to avoid anything. There were no skid marks on the road, which tells us that Reynolds didn't try to apply his breaks. He purposely drove the car off the bridge."

"Why are the windows being open or closed important?" Adiva asks.

"I'll need your help," Tony responds, motioning to me. I display an animation of a car on the bridge.

"This shows what happens when a car goes into the water with the windows open" Tony continues. "It sinks quickly and immediately fills with water. Reynolds drowned before anyone could get to him. Professor, can we see the second animation?"

Tony pauses while I display a new simulation.

"This shows what happens if the windows are closed," Tony continues. The students see that the car remains afloat for almost three minutes before it slips completely under the water. The animation then shows the car as it sinks below the waterline to the bottom of the river.

"If the windows were closed, there could still be enough air in the car for Reynolds to live long enough to be rescued. By opening the windows, he made it impossible for anyone to get to him in time."

"But he was a music teacher, not a scientist," James says. "He wouldn't know enough about the car's buoyancy and air pockets to open the windows before he turned into the water."

"Do you have anything else that would indicate suicide?" Kayla inquires.

"We talked to his girlfriend. Reynolds had just been laid off from his job and didn't appear to have any prospects locally. She's a rising star at WTAM. Leaving the area to be with him would be a major blow to her career. He was probably depressed, though we have no way to prove that. His depression could have caused him to kill himself."

Tony then displays an official looking report. "We brought the car to our lab. Our technicians went over every inch of it. We found no mechanical problems that would cause it to suddenly turn and go into the river."

145

Emanuel

"Sheriff, can we see the full report?" As usual, Judy has been fiddling with her phone throughout the entire discussion, but I know she heard every word.

Tony scrolls the document slowly so that Judy can read it.

"Can we get a look at the car?" Judy asks.

"We can," Tony replies. "The car's in our garage, which is about a mile down the road, on the right. You can't miss it. Let me call over there so my guys can get it ready for us."

I turn to the class. "Let's meet there in half an hour."

"I may be a few minutes late," Judy says. "I need to go home and change."

After Judy leaves, Adiva turns to Kayla. "She's probably going home to put on a hazmat suit, so she doesn't ruin her perfect nails or mess her hair." Both girls laugh good naturedly.

* * *

We had been standing around William's car for approximately ten minutes. Tony's technicians are explaining how they examine a car for evidence, when Judy walks in. Everyone gapes.

"What the—?" Diego exclaims.

Judy is dressed in a car mechanic's coveralls, with a bandana wrapped around her head, and carrying a large tool box. "Sheriff, can we get the car up on a lift?" Judy turns to her classmates. "Don't look so surprised. My grandfather owns an auto repair shop. When I was growing up, I spent many days after school and weekends in his shop. The men who worked there adopted me as their mascot and taught me about auto mechanics. Now, let's take a closer look at this puppy."

With the car up on the lift, Judy pulls one tool after another out of her box. After about half an hour she's finished. "Sheriff, your guys are right. There's nothing wrong mechanically. Did you inspect the computer chips? I didn't see anything in your report about them."

Tony looks at his two technicians. They both shake their heads, appearing somewhat confused.

"Is it OK if I pull some of these chips out and take them back to our lab?" Judy asks. "They might shed some light on what happened."

"Go ahead, young lady," Tony replies. "Computer chips in cars. What will we see next?"

"Doc," Judy turns to me, "can I bring a guest to the next workshop? I think he can help us."

"Sure." My students' ingenuity and creativity never cease to amaze me. As the song from the Broadway show, *The King and I*, states, *if you become a teacher, by your pupils you'll be taught.*

* * *

For the following week's workshop, I had offered to get another gift pack from the Third Avenue Deli, but the students talked me out of it. *One round of heartburn*, they said, *was enough.* Diego brought Mexican delicacies and Alex delivered the sweetest strawberries and blueberries I've ever tasted. Judy is standing at the instructor's podium.

"I want to introduce Mr. Rick Oleander," Judy says, gesturing to a tall, distinguished looking gentleman, who appears to be in his mid-thirties to early forties. "Mr. Oleander worked for my grandfather and is one of the men who taught me auto mechanics. He went on to earn a bachelor's and master's degree in Automotive Engineering. He currently works for Advanced Automotive Services, a consulting firm that specializes in developing the technology we will find in the cars of the future, such as self-driving cars. After our last workshop, I asked grandpa if he had contact information for Mr. Oleander. I knew Mr. Oleander would be able to help us. And, a little secret I've never told anyone. When I was eleven years old, I had a mad crush on Mr. Oleander."

Emanuel

Rick Oleander approaches the speaker's podium and smiles at Judy. "And another secret, all the men in the shop had a crush on you."

I'd never seen Judy blush before.

He turns to the class. "When Judy invited me to help with your case, I told her that my company usually charges $450 an hour for my services. She told me that she couldn't raise that kind of money but did mention the snack table you guys always have. That was enough for me. "Now, let's look at these chips Judy pulled from that car." Oleander places one of the chips into a slot on the side of the computer. Green text on a black background flashes on the screen. "As many of you know, there are multiple computers that control functions in today's cars. Can anyone name one?"

As usual, Alex is first to speak. "Low tire pressure."

"Correct. There's a computer chip that monitors your tires. When the pressure goes below a given level, you get a warning. Anything else?"

"How about that message that comes up in my car, telling me I'm due for service?" one of the deputies asks.

"You're right. Now, the one we're looking at is the code that monitors the car's steering mechanism. Let me bring up an application my company uses to test and evaluate these systems." Oleander presses a few buttons. "Does anyone see something that might cause us to raise questions about this code?"

"Some of the text displays in red," James replies.

"Yes, and that indicates the code was not part of the original program. Someone hacked into the chip and installed additional instructions. Judy, do you want to tell the class what we found?"

Judy is still blushing. "Mr. Oleander invited me to his office. We ran a series of tests and found the code displaying in red which disengaged the steering mechanism, so the driver could not control the car. It

then turned the wheel, to steer the car off the bridge."
Judy looked at Oleander.

"Keep going, young lady, you're doing just fine. What else did we find?"

Judy removes the chip and replaces it with another. This one also has a small amount of red text embedded with the green. "We discovered that all four windows had been automatically rolled down and then disabled. Mr. Reynolds had no control over the steering wheel or the windows when it went into the river."

"But how did the hacker know when the car would be on the bridge?" James asks.

Judy places a third chip into the computer. By now the class knows that the red text means that something's wrong with the code. "This is the disk that controls the GPS system. It monitors the car's location. The red code sent a signal to the other chips to take control of the steering and window functions when Mr. Reynolds entered the Alafia Bridge. It triggered the windows to open and the steering mechanism to turn the car into the river."

"Hold on," one of Tony's deputies says. "We examined the steering and window systems. We didn't find them locked."

"I can answer that," Oleander replies. "Each one of the hacks contained a reset command. Chips in cars are well insulated, allowing them to operate in conditions such as heat, cold, even when submerged in water. After the car hit the river, the reset mechanism triggered, and control returned to the driver. By then it was too late. The car went under and Reynolds drowned."

James' body relaxes in his chair. He appears to be relieved. "We now know Mr. Reynolds didn't commit suicide. Someone hacked his car, but we don't know who did it, how it was done, or why."

Emanuel

"I have an idea about the *how*," I say. "Sheriff, did you recover Reynolds' phone?"

"We did. I have it right here." Tony grabs the phone from an evidence shelf.

"Was it still in working order after being in the water?"

"Our lab guys were able to get it in working order."

"One way the car's chips could have been hacked was from software on the phone. Let's see if we can find code that may have been transferred to the car's computer systems."

I plug William's phone into my computer terminal. Data flashes on the lab's monitors. It takes less than two minutes for James and Diego to almost simultaneously find what we are looking for, red letters in the program code of an email he received.

* * *

"This is going to be fun, dear," Deb says, as we get into our golf cart for the Southern Heritage Day parade and picnic.

"You're a genius," I reply, "coming up with a way for two native New Yorkers to enjoy the day's festivities."

"I talked with Beatrice to ensure no one would be insulted. She laughed when I told her my plan, saying it is a great way to meld cultures, although she did make me grovel."

Deb had done all the work. I back our golf cart out of our driveway and head toward the tennis courts, where the parade is to begin. We're fifth in line. Harrison and Beatrice pull up behind us, their cart decorated with Tulane University banners. Harrison stares at our cart for a moment, then breaks out laughing. "Lionel, Deb, you're definitely going to win the award for most original design."

Deb has our cart decked out with banners from her alma mater, Pace University. On the back is a large sign, *On the Southern Tip of Manhattan.*

150

We are ready to begin the parade when I see a car from the Sheriff's Department enter our parking lot. Tony and one of his deputies exit the car. I know why he's here.

Tony approaches Harrison and pulls handcuffs from his belt. "Harrison Forsythe, you're under arrest for the murder of William Reynolds."

* * *

My students sit attentively as I enter the lab. James had supplied the snacks, wang wang snow cookies, sugar coated Haws, and pan-fried onion pancakes.

"Hey, Prof," Diego says, "we heard the Doctor was arrested. What happened?"

"Since James has a special interest in this case, I asked him to help me analyze Mr. Reynolds' phone. James, tell them what we found?"

"Thanks, Doc." James turns toward the class. "Take out your phones." Everyone takes their phones out of their pockets. Naturally, Judy already had hers in her hand. "Now, what is the first thing you do when you get into your car?"

"Set my phone on the dashboard and turn on my tunes," Alex replies. "I don't want to listen to that stuff on the radio."

"Any of you not do that?" No one's hand goes into the air. "Doc, tell them what you saw."

"You all remember the workshop when Mr. Reynolds spoke to us about DNA. He was ill, and Dr. Forsythe suggested that they meet at the clinic. The doctor and I walked with William to his car. We both saw him set his phone on the dashboard, even before he started the motor. That led me to the conclusion that the most likely way the hacked software got into Mr. Reynolds' car's computer system was through his phone. James, why don't you pick up the story?"

"Using Mr. Oleander's software, we found the code used to hack Mr. Reynolds' car was embedded in a strep

151

throat prescription document attached to an email the doctor sent to Mr. Reynolds. We know that Dr. Forsythe, a white hat hacker, knows all about embedding code in files. Sheriff, I believe you discovered our next bit of evidence."

"I did," Tony replies, "but I'll need your help with the computer. I'm still all thumbs with that thing. The information James and the professor obtained from Mr. Reynolds' phone enabled us to get an arrest warrant and the right to search the doctor's phone and computer. James, can you show that DNA thing, and explain it?"

James accesses three files, each containing DNA analysis, and displays them on the lab's screens. "The DNA analysis on the left-hand side and center of the screen are both Mr. Reynolds'. We found the first one on Mr. Reynolds' computer and the second on Dr. Forsythe's computer. It appears the doctor sent a swab for analysis the same day he examined Mr. Reynolds. The sheriff questioned Dr. Forsythe's medical assistant. She told him she believes the doctor took two swabs when he examined Mr. Reynolds, but only gave her one to send to the lab. We're assuming he sent the second one for DNA analysis."

"But why would he do that?" Adiva asks.

"The sheriff's warrants gave him access to the doctor's financial records." James displays a copy of a credit card statement and points to an entry. "As you can see, the charge is for two DNA analyses. Doctor Forsyth obtained a copy of both his and Mr. Reynolds' DNA."

James shows a fourth document on the screens. "Take a look at this DNA comparison report, which we found on the doctor's computer. It clearly shows that Dr. Forsythe is closely related to Mr. Reynolds, probably his father. I had a hunch about that after we displayed the age progression application at our workshop a few weeks ago. When we ran our pictures through the software, I noticed that an older Mr. Reynolds looked a lot like the doctor.

Mr. Reynolds also ran a picture of his mother to see what she looked like when he was born."

"I remember saying that Mrs. Reynolds hadn't changed much," Kayla offers.

"I think the doctor noticed both pictures," James continues. "He recognized Mrs. Reynolds and saw how Mr. Reynolds' age progression looked like him."

"And one more bit of evidence," Tony says. "When we interviewed Reynolds' mother, she told us that she visited Dr. Forsyth when she became ill. I'm sure he recognized her, and the images and the DNA report convinced him that Mr. Reynolds was his son."

James continues. "When the Prof. introduced Mr. Forsythe at the workshop, he said he graduated Temple University, which is in Philadelphia, in 1985. Mr. Reynolds told us that his mother was raped thirty-five years ago in Philadelphia. The time line and place fit."

"But why would the doctor kill Mr. Reynolds?" Alex inquires. "You'd think he'd want to get to know his long-lost son?"

"You're being naïve," Kayla responds. "Do you remember what Mr. Reynolds told us about his birth?"

"Oh, yeah, his mother was raped, but I don't think he could be sent to jail for the rape, can he, sheriff? The statute of limitations has long passed."

"You're right," Tony replies, "but our investigation unearthed some additional evidence. Professor, do you want to show everyone what we found?"

"The doctor's wife, Beatrice, was extremely proud of her southern ancestor, Confederate General James Longstreet. I also remembered a discussion I had with a friend of mine, Drew Delacroix. What I'm about to display may be somewhat disturbing, but it's important that you see it." I show Beatrice's posts on social media and Neighborchat, clearly showing her disapproval of miscegenation, and her racist attitude. "It would be bad

153

enough if she discovered her husband had a son from a woman he raped thirty-five years ago, but to learn the woman was black would send her over the edge."

"Which gets us to our final piece of evidence," Tony says. "When we identified the doctor as our prime suspect, and your professor told me how his wife would feel if she learned about Mr. Reynolds, I decided to take a closer look into their marriage. I found that she inherited a significant amount of money from her parents and her first husband. He entered the marriage with very little. Dr. Forsythe earned a decent living in his career, but he hadn't saved much. I suspected they might have a prenuptial agreement. I was right. If they divorce, he would be left with little more than the clothing on his back. He couldn't take a chance that William would learn that the doctor was his father."

I watch the Tech Squad leave the lab, Diego again going into his Mohammed Ali *we're the greatest* mimicry. I turn to Tony. "Maybe this generation is doing a better job than ours learning to accept and enjoy racial and ethnic differences."

"I hope so."

MURDER TIMES TWO

There's an ongoing debate in the field of higher education regarding the relative value of degrees in the STEM disciplines (science, technology, engineering, and math) and the liberal arts, which include history, literature, art, drama, and music. At Tampa Bay Community College, we insist that students study both. To graduate, the STEM students in my *Tech Squad* workshop must earn one-third of their credits in the liberal arts fields. In our next case one of my students used knowledge she gained from one of these courses to help solve two murders.

* * *

Sarah Powell and Miriam Holder stand in the aisle of Delta Airlines flight #2137 that had just completed taxiing to gate B24 at Atlanta's Hartsfield-Jackson International Airport.

"Be sure to check the overhead bins for your personal belongings before you deplane," the flight attendant says.

Miriam smiles as she remembers a George Carlin comedy routine where he asks why airlines use the term deplane. "We don't detrain," the comedian said, "or decar, or deboat. Why do we deplane?" She always enjoyed Carlin's standup act.

The plane's door swings open and the passengers exit into the terminal. The two women walk swiftly to the area where they retrieve their luggage and leave the airport. Ten minutes later the Ritz Carlton courtesy van to pull up. The driver greets the waiting passengers and places their baggage in the back of the van. The seven travelers

155

take their seats. Miriam sits in the first row, Sarah in the third. The women do not know each other, but these two strangers on Flight # 2137 will be inextricably linked for the rest of their lives.

The trip to the hotel takes twenty minutes. The two women register and head to their rooms, Sarah on the third floor, Miriam on the ninth. They unpack, freshen up, and prepare for their four-day mini vacation, Sarah free from responsibility and Miriam just free.

* * *

At 2:00 PM Miriam enters the elevator and presses the button for the lobby. The elevator stops at the third floor, and Sarah enters.

"Weren't you on the flight from Tampa?" Sarah asks.

"I was, and we rode the van together." The elevator door opens, and the women exit into the hotel's luxurious lobby. "By any chance are you here for the Interknit Conference."

The Interknit Conference is an annual gathering of people, mostly women, who enjoy knitting.

"I am. You too?" Sarah replies. "Have you attended before?"

"No, this is my first time."

"I attended two years ago in Denver. I missed last year. You'll love it. You on your way to registration? The instructions say it's in the Grand Ballroom."

"Lead the way."

The two women leave the elevator and walk to the registration area. Miriam's eyes open wide. Most of the room is filled with vendors displaying yarns and knitting tools.

"This is like Dorothy when she opened the door after her home landed in Oz," she exclaims, "all these colors, magenta, turquoise, golden rod, ivory, espresso, and stitch markers, row counters, yarn winders, needles, knitting bags and crochet hooks of all shapes and sizes. It's overwhelming."

156

Miriam and Sarah approach the registration booth, which is located along the wall at the far-right side of the room, sit at adjoining computer terminals, and begin entering the necessary information.

Miriam stops on the fifth entry screen and turns toward Sarah. "What's this *KnitzyKnews* thing?" she asks? "Do I want to sign up."

"*KnitzyKnews* is a blog. Knitters all over the world subscribe. We exchange all types of information about knitting, or anything else, for that matter. When I have a question, I post it and usually get an answer in a day or two. You can also create private chat rooms which only people who have been invited can access. I'm a member of one called *Warm Weather Knitting* for those of us who live in states like Florida where we don't need heavy wools. I'll invite you, if you like."

"I'd appreciate that."

The two women exit the Grand Ballroom and sit on the couches in the hotel's main lobby. They open an envelope which contains information about the workshops and presentations, deciding which ones they want to attend. Sarah notices Miriam suddenly look upward toward the mezzanine level above the balcony. Sarah immediately follows Miriam's glance. They both see an athletic woman wearing a uniform with a holstered pistol around her waist.

Sarah gently places her hand on Miriam's arm. "We'll probably see more people like that during our stay," she says. "Ever since the mass shooting in Las Vegas, hotels have increased security, especially when they host international events like this one. They're here to keep us safe. We'll probably never interact with a member of the security staff." How wrong she is.

* * *

Virginia DeRento takes one last look at the hotel lobby from her mezzanine level vantage point. Her shift is

Emanuel

almost over. She has been working for SBT Security Services for a little over six months, ever since she retired from the Army. She expects this assignment will be easy. After all, who'd want to disrupt a group of women at a knitting conference? Of course, you never know. Random shooters will pick anyone, even people who look like their grandmother.

At 4:00 she descends the stairway which will take her to the lobby and spots the tall black man coming toward her. "All's quiet, Charlie," she says. "You got the 4-12 shift?"

"I do," Charlie Saxton replies.

"Well, keep those blue hairs safe."

Virginia continues down the stairs, exits the hotel, goes to her car in the parking garage, and drives to her small, one-bedroom apartment. She's been living here since she retired, and still has most of her clothes in suitcases and cardboard boxes. Tomorrow's her day off. Maybe she'll unpack, and then again, maybe not. She's about half way through a good mystery, one she found in a used bookstore. The pages are a little ragged and stained, but the two-dollar price fit right into her budget.

Virginia isn't hungry. Free meals are one advantage of working hotel security. She sits in the chair she bought from Goodwill when she rented the apartment, reads about fifty pages of her mystery, and then it's time for the game. She grew up rooting for the Braves. It was the one thing she and her father shared. When she was seven, she decided she wanted to play for them when she grew up. When she was eleven, she was devastated and cried for three days when her father told her only men play in the major leagues.

She falls asleep in the fifth inning, wakes at about 2 o'clock in the morning, and immediately grabs her phone to check the baseball scores. *Great,* she thinks. *They won. They're only two games out of first place. There are*

158

two weeks left in the season. Maybe this year they'll make the playoffs. She nods off again.

She wakes at about 8:00, makes herself bacon, eggs and toast, grabs the book she's reading, a blanket, and folding chair, and drives to the park next to the hotel. She'll finish her book and then enjoy the rest of the day in the great outdoors.

It's about 9:30 when Virginia looks up from her reading just in time to see what could be a very bad accident. Two women are walking in the pathway about ten feet in front of her. A young man riding a bicycle is about thirty feet behind them. He's wearing headphones and appears unaware that he is about to collide with the two women. Virginia's military training kicks in. She springs toward the two women and knocks them out of the way just in time to avoid an accident. The bicycler just speeds by, as if nothing had happened. The three women are sprawled on the ground. Fortunately, they all landed on the grass, not the pavement.

"You OK?" Virginia asks.

"I think so," Sarah replies then, looking toward her companion, "Miriam, what about you?"

"I'm fine. What happened?"

"I think this lady just saved us from a terrible accident. Are you OK ma'am?"

Virginia sits up and brushes herself off. "I'm OK."

"Say," Miriam says, "I recognize you? Didn't I see you at the hotel yesterday?"

"Probably, I'm working security for a large knitting conference they're having."

"And we're two of the knitters you're guarding. You can tell your boss you are doing your job, even when you're off duty." All three women laugh as they get up and brush themselves off.

"Are you enjoying your stay?" Virginia asks.

"I am," Sarah and Miriam reply, almost simultaneously. "There aren't any workshops we want to attend this morning," Miriam continues, "so we decided to get some fresh air. Do you knit?"

Sarah and Miriam sit on a bench and Virginia pulls her lounge chair over to them.

"No, it isn't a hobby many women in the Army take up."

"You're in the Army?" Sarah asks.

"I was. Just retired after twenty years."

"What was the Army like?" Miriam inquires.

For the next two hours the three women talk about their lives as if they were old friends. Virginia talks about her lonely childhood. "My parents were somewhat cold, both to me and to each other. I think I was an accident and the only reason they married was because my mother was pregnant. My father and I shared a love of baseball, but nothing else. I don't remember either of them ever hugging me or kissing me. Even as a child, I sensed something was wrong and I vowed I would never be this way when I married and had children."

"Do you have children?" Miriam asks.

In her thirty-nine years Virginia had never met anyone who really appeared interested in her, or her life. Maybe this is why she feels comfortable opening up to these two women. "No, when I was about sixteen, I recognized I wasn't like the other girls. By then I was over six feet tall. None of the boys ever asked me out, but I didn't care. I found I was more attracted to some of the girls in my class. I never had any friends. I did enjoy reading," she says, showing the mystery novel she's holding. "It was my escape. Three days after I graduated high school, I went to the Army recruiting office. They signed me up immediately. By the time I was eighteen, I was six-foot-three and weighed just under two hundred and twenty pounds. I later learned that recruiters are always under pressure to fill slots in the all-volunteer Army and there is additional emphasis on getting women to sign up.

When I told Sergeant Bailey, I still remember his name, that I could bench press two hundred and fifty pounds, he must have felt he had died and gone to recruiter heaven."

Virginia can see from the looks on the faces of her new-found friends that they appear truly interested in what she is telling them. They aren't just being polite.

"You must have liked the Army," Miriam says. "You stayed in for twenty years."

"It was OK. I never really made any friends. I think the guys resented me because I was stronger than they were, and the women didn't know what to make of me. I was different. I was once allowed to box on our base's men's boxing team. That was a mistake. I had three bouts, winning all three, two by knockout. I was pulled from the team after that. I guess the men's egos were bruised—."

"—among other things," Sarah says. All three women laugh.

"What did you do in the Army?" Miriam asks.

"Infantry. I did tours in both Iraq and Afghanistan. My last three years I was an instructor at Fort Hood, Texas, teaching weaponry. These recruits may not have liked me, and maybe even saw me as strange, but they realized that what I taught them might save their lives one day."

"So, you taught them how to shoot?"

"And use knives, grenades, rocket launchers, and even their bare hands. When in combat, you use whatever you have."

"So now, you're a security guard. Is that what you plan to do from now on?" Miriam inquires.

"I'm not sure what I want to do. I'll probably go back to school to learn a trade. There's not a great demand in today's business world for someone whose most recognizable skill is killing people. My military benefits will pay for my education. After I finish school, I think I want to start my own company, but that takes money.

Emanuel

I'm going to need some way to get start-up cash for my business. But how selfish of me, I've spent—," Virginia looks at her watch, "—almost a half-hour talking about myself. I'd like to know more about you."

Sarah and Miriam talk about their lives and the challenges they face at home. Virginia is pleased that they are both readers and they talk about their favorite books. They ask about the one Virginia is reading that day and appear fascinated as she describes the plot.

"I think I'd like to read that book," Sarah says, glancing at Miriam.

"Me too," Miriam replies.

When Miriam and Sarah stand to return to the hotel and Virginia to her apartment, all three believe they have an answer to their problems, and life will be better moving forward. Only one is correct.

* * *

"Damn it, Richard, that's the third home health aide who's quit, each one saying they can't stand being in a room with you." Sarah Powell knows she must calm down. Dr. Jamison told her that her high blood pressure is caused, in part, by her resentment of her husband. Her recent trip to Atlanta was a brief respite, but now she must confront reality.

Richard has always been demanding. They had both worked before they retired to Sun Coast Shores. He was a middle manager for an insurance company. She had been a surgical nurse. She also cared for the house, cooked, cleaned, and took most of the responsibility for raising their three children. He came home, went into his man-cave, sprawled on his leather couch, and did very little. There were times, after working a double shift, when she wanted to come home and collapse, but couldn't. She had household chores to complete. He even expected her to appear appreciative just because he mowed the lawn once a week and occasionally emptied the dishwasher.

She thought life would be easier when they retired, and, for a while, it was. He had one of the lowest handicaps in the golf club and played at least three times a week. She enjoyed activities at their clubhouse and worked out at the community gym. She had been an athlete in high school and college and took pride in being in excellent physical shape. Even at age sixty-two, men still glanced her way at the pool and when she wore shorts while out shopping. Richard still expected her to cook and clean. When he came home from the golf course, he hit the couch and wanted to be served. Life was good, if not great. Their pensions, savings, and investments provided a comfortable, if not luxurious, lifestyle.

Everything changed six months ago when he fell and broke his hip. He now needs a walker around the house and a golf cart when he goes out. His orthopedist told her that Richard has degenerative arthritis of the hip. He can't play golf any more, although he rides his golf cart up to the first tee every evening at about 6:00 PM, rain or shine. He says the few minutes he spends there helps him forget that he will never be the same again.

"Why should we spend the money on a home health aide?" Richard demands. "You can help me. When we married, we said we'd be there in sickness and in health. Well, this is sickness. I expect you to be there. Anyway, don't I let you go to your Tuesday evening knitting group at the clubhouse. You leave before I go for my ride and you come back long after I get home. It's not easy for me to get into and out of my cart by myself, but I do it, just so you can have a girl's night out. At least, *you say* you're knitting. I wouldn't be surprised if you're meeting a man."

Sarah can feel her blood pressure rising. She bristles when he says he *lets her go* to her knitting group, as if she needs his permission, and she has never been unfaithful to him. He had at least one affair, 25 years ago.

Emanuel

He doesn't know that she found out and she's never mentioned it. "First of all, we can easily afford the aide. Our home health policy pays 80% of the cost. And second, I don't need your permission." Sarah wants to slap the son-of-a-bitch, but she holds back.

She's talked about how demanding Richard is with the other women in the knitting group. Richard's refusal to accept help from a home health aide had almost derailed her plans to attend the Interknit Conference in Atlanta last month. Fortunately, her daughter was able to stay with him while she was away. Deborah and her father are close. He's always on his best behavior when his little girl's around. She has no idea the kind of man he is when she's gone.

Many of her friends have similar issues with their husbands. They often mention the advice of the serenity prayer, *God, grand me the serenity to accept the things I cannot change, the courage to change the things I can, and the wisdom to know the difference.* Most of the women have resolved to accept what they cannot change. She knows that Richard's condition and demanding personality aren't going to improve. She can't change that, but soon it will be time to change one thing she can, very soon.

* * *

Miriam gently pulls the trigger. "Bulls eye," her husband, Fred, shouts, "that's three in a row."

"Can we go now?" she begs. "I don't want to do this anymore."

"You missed time at the range when you went on that damn trip to Atlanta last month and, anyway, I paid for an hour, and we have fifteen minutes left," he replies. "Keep shooting."

"Why do I need a gun, anyway?"

"So, you can protect yourself when you're on the road and I'm not around."

Miriam and Fred have had this argument before and, as usual, he wins. Since earning a master's degree in computer technology twenty-three years earlier, she has worked for the Florida Department of Education, traveling throughout the state, showing school districts and state colleges how to apply for state and federal loans and grants to purchase computer hardware and software applications and integrate them into their curriculum. She often meets with administrators and teachers at night.

"School parking lots are dangerous, especially after dark," Fred continues. "If one of those punks comes at you, it's going to be either you or him."

"I always carry pepper spray in my purse. That should be more than enough." Miriam has never told Fred that she leaves the gun in her car when she goes to one of her meetings. Schools are no place for guns.

"Not against them. When one of those big gorillas comes at you—."

Miriam pulls back. She hates when Fred uses a term like *gorillas*. She knows exactly what he means.

"—OK, big guys come at you, you'll be glad I taught you to use a gun."

Miriam continues shooting, under Fred's watchful eye.

It's 10:30 at night as the couple heads home. Miriam sits quietly in the passenger seat and tightens her seat belt. Fred has never been a cautious driver and, lately, he has become less so, tailgating, zipping around a car he thinks isn't moving fast enough, and blasting his horn at the vehicle in front of him when the light turns green. She feels less safe with him than in any school parking lot.

She dreads what's going to happen when they get home. They've been married for twenty-one years. The first two years their lovemaking was great, well, if not great, at least good. The next fifteen years she just laid back and hoped it would be over, quickly, but the last

165

three—. By the time he rolls over and falls asleep, she's in pain. She knows this can't continue. She also knows that tomorrow morning, at breakfast, he'll be contrite and possibly amenable to what she wants to talk about.

* * *

"Good morning," Miriam says in the most cheerful voice she can muster, as Fred joins her for morning coffee. Fred mumbles something, approaches the Keurig coffee maker, brews a cup, and taps a few keys on his phone. She knows not to broach the topic until he's checked the scores. He hasn't lived in New York since they married, but he still follows his beloved Yankees.

Fred smiles. "They won and are still two games ahead of the Red Sox."

Good, Miriam thinks, *this is the perfect time to bring up the floors*. "Can we talk about something?"

"Sure."

"The carpeting in the bedrooms is looking ragged. I think we should replace it, maybe with laminate floors."

"Are you kidding?" he shouts. "That'll cost thousands. You just spent all that money on that damn knitting thing in Atlanta. Now you want to waste our dough on floors. Absolutely not!"

She knew he would say no. That's always his reaction whenever she wants to spend money, but she didn't expect him to be so adamant. Damn him.

He was so generous when they were dating. He took her on a cruise and proposed under a full moon at sea. But after they married—. She entered the marriage with a savings account of $8,000. Her biggest regret is that she agreed to merge their finances. Now, she must beg him any time she wants to spend money.

"Can we, at least talk about it when you get back from your business trip to Miami?"

"Yeah, OK."

Miriam knows he doesn't mean it. She isn't surprised. *Why do I imagine this time will be different*, she thinks?

166

Anything he wants, like the tennis court he built in the back yard, he gets. If it's something I want, like the new floors, the answer is 'no'. Well, that's about to change.

That afternoon, when Fred is out of the house, she logs onto the appropriate application on her phone and types, *I'm in.*

* * *

"It's Tuesday," Richard says. "So, I guess you're going to that dumb knitting group of yours."

Sarah has learned to ignore those little digs of his. He resents her doing anything but caring for him. Still, it grates on her when he refers to her *dumb* knitting group. "Yeah," Sarah replies, "I'm going to my dumb knitting group, and I suppose you're going to your dumb first tee."

Sarah watches her husband pull his golf cart out of the driveway. Once she's assured he hasn't forgotten anything and is on his way, she grabs her phone, accesses the appropriate application, and types the confirming information. She's been doing this every Tuesday evening for the past three weeks. This time she sees what she has been waiting for, one word, *tonight.* Sarah pockets her phone and heads to the clubhouse.

"What's on the menu tonight?" Sarah asks, as she sits at the table in the clubhouse Bistro with the five other women in her knitting group. They always meet at 7:00 for dinner, and then retire to the Crafts' Room for their meeting.

"Filet of Sole Almondine," Adele Becker replies, "with asparagus and apple pie for dessert."

"Great," Sarah replies.

"You seem in especially good spirits this evening," Adele notes.

"I've never felt better."

* * *

The driver of the blue Chevy sedan pulls into the 7-Eleven parking lot. She takes her phone from her purse, accesses the appropriate application, and types *Tonight*. She exits, locks her car, and begins walking. She's scouted the area and did a dry run the day before. It's almost a mile to the golf course. On foot, it will take about twenty minutes to get there. She walks along a heavily used path. Even if the cops discover she used this path and try to identify footprints, they'll have no reason to pick hers out from the others.

She would have preferred to drive, but too many people have surveillance videos attached to their homes. It's beginning to get dark and she assumes no one will be on the path. If she encounters anyone along the way, she'll turn back and try again another day. She looks up. The sky's clear and there's a full moon. This will make her job easier.

* * *

It's a half mile from Richard's and Sarah's house to the 7-Eleven. Richard exits his golf cart and walks slowly to the door, aided by his walker. A man leaving the convenience store holds the door for Richard.

"Thank you," Richard says, tipping his hat to the man.

"Good evening, Mr. Powell," the man behind the counter says. "Your usual?"

"Yup."

Priya knows that Richard takes an extra-large cup of coffee with cream and four sugars. He pours the coffee, takes it to the counter, processes Richard's credit card, and carries the coffee as he walks with his customer to the cart.

"I appreciate your help, Priya." Richard pulls a dollar bill from his pocket and gives it to the convenience store clerk. "Since I broke my hip and need this damn walker, I have difficulty carrying stuff to the cart."

Richard exits the parking lot and heads to the first tee.

* * *

"Evening, Ralph," Richard says, as he passes the clubhouse.

"How you feeling?" Ralph responds.

"Terrible. I've got this bum hip and the doc tells me it's something called *degenerative*. It means I'm never going to play golf again."

"Look, I know you can't play, but you're always welcome to join us for a round. We'd love to have you tell us everything that's wrong with our game."

"Thanks, I appreciate the offer, but I couldn't. I'd keep remembering those days when I used to beat you guys regularly. It would be too painful."

"I remember those days, too, but you're always welcome. We play every Wednesday morning. Our tee time is 8:00."

* * *

The woman's hike is uneventful. There's no one on the path. She's at the first tee in twenty-five minutes. She finds a spot where she can kneel behind a bench and not be seen, no more than thirty feet from the tee. She pulls surgical gloves, a gun, and silencer from the fanny pack around her waist, dons the gloves, and attaches the silencer onto the barrel. Richard pulls up on his golf cart, stops, and lifts the styrofoam coffee cup out of the holder. *Perfect*, she thinks. *His head is silhouetted against the moon.* She aims and shoots. The cup falls to the ground, followed by the man. She looks around. This is when she is most vulnerable. If anyone is nearby, she will have to leave quickly. She sees no one. She picks up the warm shell casing, tucks it in her fanny pack, and waits a few minutes to ensure nobody heard the shot. The man doesn't move. She approaches her victim and sees blood gushing from his head. Standing far enough from the body to ensure that blood and brain matter can't reach her and get on her clothes, she shoots again, just to ensure he's dead.

She retrieves the second shell casing then quickly turns, removes the gloves, places them and the shell casing in her fanny pack, and retraces her steps along the path. It's dark. Although she assumes no one will be on the path this late, she doesn't feel comfortable until she's in her car. She steers away from the 7-Eleven parking lot, pulls over just prior to the interstate on ramp, grabs her phone from her purse, accesses the appropriate application, and types *Done*.

I'll have to get rid of the gun, she thinks, *but that will have to wait*.

* * *

After dessert dishes are removed, the women retire to their meeting.

"Have you completed that sweater you've been knitting for Richard?" one of the knitters asks Sarah.

Sarah hesitates for a moment. "Eh—, no. I put it aside last week. I'm working on a shawl for myself. You know how cold it is in restaurants, and I always seem to be seated under a vent."

Sarah turns to Shirley Greenberg. Shirley organized the knitting group two years ago and had become the de facto leader. "So, what are we working on this evening?"

"Wool socks," Shirley replies. "We're knitting them for our grandchildren up north. The temperature's hitting eighty-five here in Florida, but it's still chilly up there." The women spend the next two hours knitting and talking.

"We've now come to the hard part," Adele Becker says, "heels."

"Oh, you mean like some of the men in this community," Claudia Gilliam replies.

The five women sitting around in a circle all laugh.

"No, heels on socks, not heels, as in husbands," Adele continues. "I've always had problems knitting heels."

"I can help with that," Sarah says. Sarah spends the next forty-five minutes showing the proper techniques.

The group breaks up at about 10:30 and Sarah heads toward the parking lot. She checks her phone as she opens her car's door. It's over. She knows what she will find when she gets home. Nothing.

Back in high school, Sarah had been in the drama club. More recently, she had performed in three shows with the Sun Coast Shores Community Theater and had learned a good deal about acting from Stuart Abbott. She knows she's going to need this skill in the next few months.

Sarah unlocks her front door, turns on the light, and walks through her house. She wants to be sure. Satisfied, she pulls her phone from her purse and dials 911. "I don't know what to do," she sobs. "He should be home by now."

"Who should be home?" the operator asks.

"My husband. Where can he be? He could be hurt."

"Calm down, ma'am. Tell me what happened."

Sarah decides that this is the time to get a little more rational. "My husband left at about 5:00 this evening. He likes to ride on his golf cart up to—," *time to get a little weepy, again,* she thinks. "—What will I do? He may be somewhere out there, hurt or something."

"OK," the operator says. "Just tell me what happened."

Sarah decides to just tell the story, now. "My husband rides every evening to the first tee in his golf cart. I was at a meeting of my knitting group. We're learning to make socks for our grandchildren, up north. You know how cold it gets up there. Anyway, he's usually back before me. I just got home and he's not here. Can you find him?"

"What's your husband's name."

"Richard. Richard Powell."

"What does he look like?"

"He's about 5'9", with a beer belly and bald. Oh, he has a mole about two inches above his left ear. I keep telling him to see a doctor. It may be skin cancer. But you know how men are. They never listen."

Emanuel

"Has your husband ever wandered off?" the operator asks.

"No, but he has been somewhat forgetful lately. Do you think that's what happened? He just wandered off?"

"We'll contact the Wanderers Patrol. It's not uncommon for people in your community to become disoriented."

Most of the residents of Sun Coast Shores are over fifty-five, many in their seventies and eighties. Some suffer from the maladies associated with aging. It's not uncommon for a person to get disoriented, often at night. The Community Association formed the Wanderers Patrol to help locate their neighbors and bring them home. When the Sheriff's Office or Community Security Watch receives a call about someone missing, they contact Jeff Bierman, the head of the patrol. The group usually finds the missing person within an hour or two.

"Oh, I feel so much better."

Sarah disconnects from the call. She knows it will look strange if she simply goes to bed, so she lies down on the couch and falls asleep. The sound of the doorbell wakes her. She looks at her watch. It's 12:35 in the morning. She opens the door.

"Mrs. Powell?"

"Yes."

"I'm Deputy Daniel Boudreau." The deputy knows that the best way to deliver the news is to be direct. "I have some bad news. We found your husband. He's been killed."

"What, —what happened? Did someone run over him with a golf cart?"

"No, he was shot."

"Where?"

"On the golf course."

Sarah again calls on her theatrical training. "Oh no," she wails "Who would do such a thing,"

172

"We will do everything we can to find out. Do you know anyone who would want to hurt him?"

"No. He was a kind man. Everyone loves him. What, how, what do I do?"

"Can I call anyone for you?"

"No, no, deputy. I don't want to disturb my neighbors this late at night. I'll just call my daughter, Deborah."

"Can she come over to stay with you?"

"No, she lives in Chicago, but she'll know what to do. She's very smart."

Deputy Boudreau is reluctant to leave this poor woman, but there's nothing else he can do for her, now. "Here's my card. If there's anything you need, just call."

"Thank you."

Sarah immediately calls Deborah and tells her what happened.

"I'll be on the first flight to Tampa in the morning. Meanwhile, please call one of your friends. You shouldn't be alone tonight."

"No, no, I'll be fine. I don't want to bother anyone."

"OK, I'll see you tomorrow, and don't talk to the police until I get there, and we find a lawyer."

"Why do I need a lawyer? I didn't do anything."

"Mom, in cases like this, the wife is always the prime suspect."

"But I didn't do anything," Sarah repeats.

"It doesn't matter, and don't say anything to the police without your attorney present."

"But, won't that make me look guilty?"

"Mom, I'll be there tomorrow and, remember, don't say anything to the police without your attorney present. I'm only looking out for your interests."

At 10:30 the next morning Sheriff Tony Maggio and Deputy Boudreau knock on Sarah's door.

Time to put on the grieving widow act, Sarah thinks as she leads the two men into her living room.

Emanuel

"Mrs. Powell," the sheriff says, "we need to talk to you about what happened to Mr. Powell."

"Oh, it's terrible. I don't know what I'm going to do." She places her head in her hands and begins to cry. *Thank you, Stuart Abbott*, she thinks, *for teaching me how actors create real tears.* "I'm just waiting for my daughter. She'll be here sometime today."

The sheriff takes out his notebook. "We just have a few questions."

"OK, what do— oh, no, I can't. My daughter says I shouldn't say anything without a lawyer, and I don't even have a lawyer even though I have nothing to hide. Is that right? I shouldn't say anything without a lawyer?"

"You have that right," the Sheriff replies.

"Can you come back when I have one?"

"We can."

Deborah arrives that afternoon at 2:30.

"Mom, is there a local attorney you can call?'

"How would I know about a lawyer. Are you sure I need one? I didn't do anything."

"You should have a lawyer present when you talk with the police."

"Wait, I may be able to find one." Sarah gets up from her chair, walks to a bookshelf, and removes a three-ring binder. "This contains a list of our Community Association's contacts. Yup, here it is, Joseph Mancuso, Attorney-At-Law. He must be the lawyer the community uses. Do you think I should call him?"

"He's probably not a criminal lawyer, but he can recommend one." Deborah dials the number listed for Mr. Mancuso. The woman answering the phone refers her to attorney Matthew Simmons. They meet with Simmons the next morning in his office and explain the situation.

"Do you have an alibi for the evening he was shot?" he asks.

"I was at the clubhouse with my knitting group from 5:00 'til 10:30. The other women in the group will tell you I was there."

"Then, that's what we'll tell the sheriff."

Attorney Simmons arranges for Sarah and Deborah to meet with Sheriff Maggio and Deputy Boudreaux at Sarah's home the next day.

Sheriff Maggio takes Sarah's statement. He learns nothing more than what Sarah had already told his deputy. Her husband had driven to the golf course the evening before, as he always did. When he wasn't home when she returned from her knitting group, she knew something was wrong and called 9-1-1. The next thing she knew Deputy Boudreau was at her door.

"Thank you, Mrs. Powell. I'd appreciate it if you would come to the police station this afternoon to identify the bod—, identify you husband. If we need anything else, we'll call."

"What will happen now, Mr. Simmons?" Sarah asks, after the sheriff and deputy leave.

"They'll contact the women in your knitting group, who will verify that you were with them the evening your husband was killed. They'll also check your financial statements to see if you paid someone to kill Mr. Powell."

"What! I didn't do any such thing."

"I know mother, but they have to check," Deborah says.

"Well, they won't find anything. I need my money to live on, and what's left will go to you when I die. Why would I hire someone—," Sarah begins to cry.

* * *

As the two police officers walk toward their car, a woman, who the sheriff guesses to be in her mid-seventies, comes running, well, more like waddling, toward them. She's dressed in what the sheriff often refers to as the Sun Coast Shores uniform, an ill-fitting camisole exposing much of her upper chest and flabby arms, and shorts that came half way between the waist and knee. This woman, and many like her, may have looked good in this outfit fifty years and seventy-five pounds ago, but now—. A second woman, dressed more conservatively, in a print dress and floppy hat, also approaches.

"Oh, officer, officer," the first woman says, brushing her hair back and then waving her arms as she approaches the deputy, "are you here to investigate poor Richard Powell's death? That's all anyone is talking about on Neighborchat. It's a tragedy, such a tragedy."

The second woman gently elbows her neighbor aside, so she can be closer to Deputy Boudreau.

The sheriff has seen this before. Women of all ages seem to gravitate to his deputy. Daniel joined the force five years ago, right out of high school, where he had been a star running back on the football team. His wavy black hair, movie star good looks, and southern accent make him what young people today call a *chick magnet*.

"Yes ma'am, that's why we're here."

"Well, it takes a lot of the burden off poor Sarah, not that she considered it a burden. Since Richard's accident, she has had to devote her life to taking care of him. That's what wives do when their husbands become ill, we take care of them. And, Sarah's a nurse, you know. Richard was lucky to have her."

The sheriff notices the first woman placing her hand on the deputy's arm and looking up at him.

"My David was sick for almost a year before he died, and I made sure he had all the care he needed. Yes, that's what wives do. In fact, Sarah was knitting a sweater for Richard at our knitting club the night he died."

"No, dear," the second woman notes. "Don't you remember, she had stopped knitting that sweater and begun a shawl for herself. I'm sure she planned to get back to the sweater but, I guess, now, she won't."

The women talk for another five minutes about how devoted Sarah was to Richard, because that's what wives do. The sheriff marvels at Deputy Boudreau's patience, as he listens and takes notes.

"Thank you, ladies," Boudreau says, when the women appear to have finished talking. "This information is very helpful."

"Well, if you need anything else young man," the first woman replies, "I live right here," pointing at the house three doors down from the Powell's.

"And I live over there," the second woman gestures to a house across the street.

The two police officers get in their car and drive off. "Looks like you have two new admirers, Daniel," the sheriff comments, softly punching the deputy's arm. "These women just love to talk with you."

"It's a gift, sir," the deputy jokes. "It's a gift."

* * *

The two weeks after Richard's death aren't easy for Sarah. It isn't the murder that bothers her; she's glad he's gone. It's pretending to be in mourning all her waking hours. After the funeral, Deborah wanted Sarah to come home with her, but Sarah declined. "What would I do in Chicago?" Sarah had asked, "sit in your house and just make you, Daryll, and your kids feel sorry for me? No, I'm better here with my friends and in my own surroundings." Deborah had insisted on spending two weeks with her in Florida, hence her need to put on an act all day.

The sheriff and Deputy Boudreau speak with Sarah three times in the two weeks that Deborah is with her, each time with her lawyer present. Sarah allows the sheriff to take a swab of her saliva, so they can test her DNA.

After her daughter leaves, Sarah can relax when she's home alone. She only has to pretend when she's with her

177

neighbors. A month after Richard's death she decides it's
OK to return to the gym and knitting group.

* * *

"Hey, numnuts," Judy says, giving James a poke in the
ribs, "didn't your mother teach you to eat dessert last."

"She did, but this praline stuff is really good."

As usual at our workshops, the Tech squad stands
around the snack table, partaking of the goodies Daniel
brought. The deputy spent his early years in Baton Rouge
and moved to Florida as a teenager. The goodies he's
brought, Cajun deviled eggs, crawfish boulettes, hush
puppies, and, for dessert, bread pudding, and praline will
definitely add to all of our waistlines.

My students settle in at their computer terminals.

"Do we have a case today, Doc?" Alex asks.

"We do."

"Is it a murder?"

"It is."

"So, we're going to figure out *who done it*?"

"Actually," Tony replies, as he displays a slide showing
the crime scene, "we think we know *who done it*. Our
problem is proving it. Let me explain. The victim is
Richard Powell, a resident of Sun Coast Shores."

"Oh Oh, Doc, they seem to be dropping like flies in your
community."

"It looks that way," Tony continues. "Anyway, as you
can see from the slide on the screen, he was shot on the
golf course. He was lying next to his golf cart, with a coffee
cup a few inches from his head. Your professor and Ms.
Morgan—," Tony points to Kayla, "—created a Photomesh
video from our crime scene photos and then developed a
Simsoft re-creation of the crime scene. See," he says,
smiling, "I'm even remembering the names of all this
techie stuff. Kayla, please explain what we found."

Kayla displays the simulation on the six screens, which
are positioned along the Sheriff Department's Tech
Center walls. "From the angle of one of the bullets, we

178

determined that the shooter was kneeling behind the bench you see on the right-hand side of the screen. That first shot hit Mr. Powell above the right ear and the second, fired from close range, penetrated his heart."

"Did you find any shell casings at the scene?" Alex asks.

"No," Tony responds. "We assume the shooter picked them up."

"So, sheriff, you say you know *who done it*?" Diego asks.

"When someone is murdered, the first person we look at is the spouse. We're almost sure his wife, Sarah, killed him."

"What makes you so certain?" Adiva inquires.

"She has a motive," Tony replies, displaying transcribed notes he and Deputy Boudreau had taken while interviewing Sarah, her neighbors, and Richard's doctor. "Apparently, he has—had something called degenerative arthritis of the hip. His condition would never improve, and she would be a caregiver for the rest of his life. According to his doctor, he was healthy in every way, other than his hip, so he could have lived another twenty or thirty years. One of the neighbors said that, since his accident, she has had to devote her life to taking care of him. That could give Mrs. Powell reason to want him gone. She may want to do more with her life than looking after Richard."

"Since we're here to try to prove she did it," James replies, "I assume you don't have enough evidence to arrest her."

"You're right. We found fingerprints and trace evidence such as hairs and fabric at the murder scene, but they didn't match anything in any criminal database. A golf course is a public area, so we'd expect to find signs of people. There were traces of Mrs. Powell on the body, but that's to be expected, since she was his wife. None of the other trace evidence points to Mrs. Powell and she has what appears to be an ironclad alibi. She was with four other women at a knitting group at the community clubhouse. All four confirm she was there."

"She could have hired someone," Adiva notes.

"If she did, we can't find him. An assassin requires payment. There are no unusual withdrawals from her bank account, at least none we're seeing. We're at a dead end."

There's a big grin on Alex's face as he ads to the inquiry. "Eh, do you think she might have had a lover? Could he have done it?"

"Come on, Alex," Diego replies, "she's as old as my grandma. People her age don't do that type of stuff."

"You're wrong, Mr. Perez." I can sense irritation in Tony's voice. "People <u>our</u> age can still do that kind of stuff. We'll have to investigate that angle. Anyway, we got warrants that give us access to their online accounts. We're hoping you guys—," Judy places her hands on her hips and glares at Tony, who smiles. "Sorry, I should have learned by now, you guys and gals, can find something."

"We'll try," Diego responds.

"Diego, maybe you can find a boyfriend or two."

My students' heads turn toward their computers and their hands move to their keyboards and mice. After about fifteen minutes Kayla raises her hand.

"I think I may have something." Judy displays a copy of the deputies transcribed notes on the computer screen. "A member of her knitting group said Mrs. Powell stopped making a sweater for her husband just before he died. Maybe she knew he wouldn't be around much longer."

"Good," Tony states. "We'll add that observation to our notes and see if it leads somewhere."

The Tech Squad continues to work for another forty-five minutes, scouring the sheriff's and deputy's interview notes and searching Sarah's and Richard's social media accounts.

"I'm not seeing much," Diego says. "They both have Facebook accounts. Mr. Powell spent time on golf web sites and Mrs. Powell often posts on something called KnitzyKnews, which appears to be a knitting blog, but that's about it." He looks toward his classmates. "Anybody find anything else?" The other members of the Tech Squad shake their heads.

"These people lead an awfully dull life," Diego notes. "No lover anywhere or anything else exciting. If I'm having trouble falling asleep one night, I'll look at their social media accounts. I'll be nodding off in minutes. But the Tech Squad never gives up. We'll solve this case for you, sheriff, after all—," Judy sighs and raises her eyebrows. She knows what's coming. "We're the greatest."

* * *

Judy and Kayla walk to their next class, Twentieth Century American Literature.

"Have you picked a book to report on?" Kayla asks.

"I have, *Gentleman's Agreement*. It's about a journalist who pretends to be Jewish, so he can research an exposé on anti-Semitism. I never experienced it, but my parents and grandparents tell me that they did. I want to learn more about it. What about you? Have you picked a book yet?"

"Not yet. I'm going to the library right after class. I think I'd like to read a good mystery."

* * *

"I'm on my way, dear. You can reach me on my cell, if you need me." Fred Holder's business takes him to various parts of Florida's west coast. Fred doesn't know that it's not a good idea to use our pet's name for all his passwords. It makes it easy for Miriam to gain access to his online accounts. She's known for over a week where he'll be staying on this trip. It took a little extra digging, but she was soon able to get the rest of the information she needed. Her plan has been put in motion.

Emanuel

"I'll see you when I get back on Thursday," he says, as he opens the door to the garage.

No, you won't, she thinks. After he leaves, Miriam lifts her phone from the dining room table, accesses the appropriate application, and enters the dates and location.

* * *

A woman wearing dark clothing and a hooded sweatshirt logs onto her phone, notes the message, finds the motel's website, and views its floorplan. *Perfect,* she thinks, *his room will be across the hallway and two doors down from the stairwell.*

She grabs a small rolling suitcase she had already prepared. It contains five pounds of rocks, four large, plastic bags, a roll of masking tape, and a complete change of clothes. She rolls the suitcase to her car and opens the trunk. She places one of the plastic bags on the floor, tapes one bag to the rear wall, and one to each of the side walls, then places the suitcase in the trunk.

Her GPS guides her to the motel. She checks her watch. It's 10:45. She was told her target always spends his evenings in a local bar and is back in his room by 11:00. He's traveling on business and needs a good night's sleep. She turns into the parking lot, pulling into a space near the stairwell door. She notes that there are no surveillance cameras and most of the outside lights are broken. She's concerned about her safety, but she made a bargain and she must deliver. If she doesn't, it will cost her.

* * *

"A round for me and my friend, here." Fred gestures to the bartender, and then to the young, well, maybe not so young, lady sitting on the stool next to him, with her hand half way between his knee and crotch. He had hoped for someone better, but it's getting late. She'll have to do.

"You from around here?" she purrs.

182

"Nah, I'm traveling on business."

Fred sees the woman's eyes light up. He knows the type. Picks a guy up in a bar and goes back to his room. $50, he guesses. He'll give her $30.

After two more drinks, he takes the woman's arm and leads her out of the bar. He thinks she said her name was Gina, or Gilda, or something. He doesn't remember. He doesn't care. It's a short walk to the motel. He'd prefer to stay at a better lodging when he travels. After all, he can expense it. But the better hotels have surveillance. He doesn't want that.

* * *

At the same time that Fred is charming his quest for the evening, a woman pulls the hood from her sweatshirt over her head. She cannot afford to be recognized. She removes a small rolling suitcase from the car's trunk and places it on the ground. She withdraws two surgical gloves from her pocket and pulls them on to her hands. She can't leave fingerprints. She wheels the suitcase to the stairwell door, which she opens, and climbs to the second floor. She checks the time; 10:50. If her information is correct, he'll be here in less than fifteen minutes and she'll be headed out by 11:30. She opens the stairwell door one inch, enough for her to see him coming. She also listens for others in the stairwell. If she hears anyone, she'll go into the hallway, pretending to be a guest. It's two minutes after 11:00 when she sees him. *Damn,* she thinks. *He's not alone.* She retraces her steps down the stairwell and out to her car. She has one more day to get the job done.

* * *

"Thank you for joining us for dinner this evening, Mrs. Holder." Being fed by vendors was a perk of Miriam's job helping Florida school districts and colleges integrate technology into their curricula. This is the second of a four-day meeting in Charlotte with Connor-McGill

183

publishing, the owner of the CompuHist education applications being adopted by many Florida school districts to teach American History. The purpose of her four-day trip is to learn about the application so she can explain it to the teachers and administrators, many of whom are barely computer literate. Miriam's job is to show the educators how to best utilize this system in their classrooms. Miriam spent the day with the Connor-McGill staff and would have preferred to go back to her hotel room, take a long, hot shower, order room service, watch TV for a while, and fall asleep, but she couldn't do that. So here she is, at 8:30 at night, having dinner, and forcing herself to appear interested in the conversation. After dinner, she returns to her hotel room and waits. She checks her phone three times before she falls asleep at about midnight.

* * *

The next evening the woman in the hooded sweatshirt retraces her route from the night before. She pulls into a parking space near the stairwell door, again pulls her sweatshirt hood over her head, and checks to see there's no one around. She removes her suitcase from her trunk, puts on her surgical gloves, carries the suitcase up one flight of stairs, opens the door about an inch, and waits, hoping he will be alone tonight.

* * *

Fred sits at the bar, again. That bitch is back and looking for another round, but he isn't interested. At age sixty-one, he needs an occasional night off and he really requires a good night's sleep. Tomorrow they're finalizing the specs on the plumbing contract he's been promised. He has to be alert. *Tomorrow night I'll need to celebrate*, he thinks. *I'm sure she'll be back, then.* He pays his tab with a credit card at 10:45 and heads to the motel.

* * *

At 11:05 the woman in the hooded sweatshirt sees him. He's alone and appears shaky on his feet, probably from his time at the bar. She pulls a double-edged knife from her purse. As he withdraws a room key from his pocket, she quickly approaches him, rolling her suitcase with her left hand, appearing to be a guest, and hiding the knife in her right. She's behind him as he opens the door to his room. She pushes him in, slams the door, drops her suitcase, and places her left hand on his shoulder, spinning him around. Fred has no time to react as she plunges the knife just below the rib cage, angling it upward and twisting, piercing the heart and lung. He falls to the floor, his head resting on the foot of the bed, blood gushing from the wound. The woman withdraws the knife and thrusts it twice more into his body. The splattering blood gets all over her and her clothes.

When she's sure he's dead, she removes the gloves and places them in her pocket. She grabs her suitcase, holding it away from her body, and walks to the end of the room, as far away from Fred's limp form as she can get. She strips down, placing the bloody clothes and shoes on the floor, about five feet from the suitcase. She goes into the bathroom and washes blood from her body. She returns to the spot where her suitcase lies, again avoiding the pool of blood, removes the clean clothes, and puts them on the bed. She puts the bloody garments and knife in the suitcase and closes it. She returns to the bathroom and washes away the remaining blood, which got on her hands when she placed the blood-stained clothes in the suitcase. She dresses, using her clean clothes. She knows she is most vulnerable for the next few minutes. She grabs her suitcase, peeks outside the door and, seeing no one, places a *Do Not Disturb* sign on the outside handle. She walks quickly to the stairwell door and descends to the empty parking lot, opens the car's trunk and places the suitcase on top of the plastic bag.

She re-sets her GPS and pulls away from the motel. She doesn't think anyone sees her and, even if they did, they'd have no reason to remember a non-distinct dark blue Toyota Corolla. After driving half an hour, she pulls into a dirt road. It's almost 12:30. There shouldn't be anyone out this time of night. She stops when she gets to the river, opens the trunk, removes and opens the suitcase, places the plastic bags over her bloody clothes, closes the suitcase, and tosses it into the river. The rocks cause it to sink immediately. The current will do the rest. She doesn't know where the suitcase will end up. The current will take it toward the gulf. She takes her phone from her purse, accesses the appropriate application, and types *Done.*

* * *

Miriam is again sitting anxiously in her hotel room after another dinner with the CompuHist instructors. She can't sleep. At a little after 1:00 AM she checks her phone—for the fifth time. She sees it. *Thank God,* she thinks, as she feels the tension leave her body. *It's over.*

* * *

The next morning Consuela passes room 203 twice, but the *Do Not Disturb* sign remains on the door. Her instructions are not to enter a room when the sign is posted. Before she leaves for the evening, she lets the desk clerk know that she was not able to get into room 203.

"I'll make a note of it," the desk clerk says. "The guest in that room is scheduled to check out tomorrow morning. You can clean it then."

* * *

"It's 9:30, where's the damn plumber?" the general contractor, Chris Mayer asks. "I've got a contract for him to sign and we're meeting with the electricians and dry wall guys later this morning. We're scheduled to start work on the apartment complex in two weeks. I need all the subs in place today."

186

"I've tried calling and texting him," Nora Mayer, his wife and partner, responds. "He was supposed to be here an hour ago."

"Do we have a backup plumbing contractor?"

"We do."

"Then call him. If that son-of-a-bitch Holder can't be on time to finalize the contract, we don't need him."

* * *

At 10:00 the next morning Consuela approaches room 203. The *Do Not Disturb* sign still displays. Her instructions are to knock, and if there is no answer, to enter the room. Her screams can be heard throughout the motel.

* * *

Charlie Evers is sitting behind the motel's reception desk when he hears Consuela's scream and immediately rushes to find her. He sees her standing outside room 203, holding her master key, sobbing, her head in her hands.

"What's wrong?"

The maid points to the door, saying nothing. Charlie takes the key, opens the door, and sees the ghastly scene inside. He gasps, immediately pulls his phone from his pocket, and dials 9-1-1. "Send someone to the Lutz Motel immediately. There's been a murder." He closes the door, walks over to Consuela, and guides her to his office.

It takes Sheriff Tony Maggio, Deputy Daniel Boudreau, the Medical Examiner, and Crime Scene Investigation (CSI) Unit approximately twenty-five minutes to get to the motel. Charlie leads them to room 203, where they see the dead man surrounded by a pool of blood. The sheriff closes the room off to allow the CSI team to do its job. The sheriff and deputy interview Charlie and Consuela in Charlie's office.

Charlie and Consuela are sitting on a maroon, overstuffed couch that has seen better days. "I didn't do anything," she sobs. "That's the way he was when I opened the door."

Charlie puts his arm over Consuela's shoulder. "We know," then, turning to Sheriff Maggio, "How can we help find out what happened?"

"Can you tell us his name and when he checked in?"

Charlie moves to his desk and presses a few buttons on his computer. "His name is Fred Holder. He checked in on Monday and said he planned to stay for three nights. He was scheduled to check out today."

"Do you know why he was here?"

"I think he had business in the area. A general contractor called yesterday asking for him. He said the guy was a plumber. Oh, something else. I worked a double shift on Monday, and I was here when he came in at about 11:00 PM. He was unsteady on his feet, like he had been drinking, and accompanied by a woman."

"Oh," Consuela says, dabbing her eyes with a handkerchief, "He had a *Do Not Disturb* sign on his door all day Wednesday. I didn't get into the room to clean."

The sheriff and deputy talk with Charlie and Consuela for another half-hour, then the sheriff's phone rings. "We'll be right there," then, turning to the deputy, "Madilyn has some preliminary information for us." The two men head to room 203. Charlie follows close behind.

"What can you tell us, Mad?" the sheriff asks.

Madilyn Grayson, the county's CSI Unit Supervisor, is making entries into her tablet. "From what we can see, the victim was stabbed multiple times by a long, probably about eight-inch, knife. The first thrust, just below the rib cage, probably killed him. The others were post-mortem. We've collected hairs and fibers. This being a motel room, we're going to find evidence from many people." Madilyn turns to Charlie. "Can you get us a list of guests who stayed in this room in the last six months."

"I can."

"Once we identify DNA from trace evidence," Madilyn continues, "we can check databases such as COTIS. We can eliminate evidence that matches someone who stayed in this room. Once you have a suspect, we should be able to compare his or her DNA with our remaining samples."

"Any idea how long he's been dead?" the sheriff asks.

"I'll know better when I get him on the table. Based on the state of rigor, I'd guess at least twenty-four hours."

The CSI team completes its work, and the Medical Examiner arranges to transport the body to the morgue. The sheriff snaps a picture of the victim on his phone and removes Holder's driver's license from his wallet, so he can notify next of kin.

"Can I clean up the room?" Charlie asks.

The sheriff glances toward Madilyn.

"Yup," she replies. "We're finished here."

The sheriff turns to his deputy. "Let's check nearby bars. It looks like he might have been there Monday night."

"Dugan's is the closest, about three blocks just north of here," Charlie notes.

"We'll start there."

* * *

"Ugh. What happened to him?" the bartender asks when the sheriff shows him Holder's picture. "He looks dead."

"He is," the sheriff says. "Was he in your bar the last few nights?"

"I do recognize him. He was here on Monday and Tuesday, but not yesterday. He had a lot to drink both nights— left a little tipsy."

"Did he leave with anyone?"

"Come to think of it, he did. He left with Gilda on Monday. She's one of our regulars, if you get my drift. She tried to pick him up again on Tuesday, but he didn't seem interested. Do you think she may have killed him?"

Emanuel

"We just want to talk with her. Do you know where she lives?"

"I don't, but she should be here tonight," the bartender notes. "Usually comes in between 8:30 and 9:00."

The sheriff turns to the deputy. "Dan, can you come back later to talk to— what's her name again?"

"Gilda," the bartender replies.

"Can you talk with Gilda? I'll notify next of kin."

"Sure, boss."

The sheriff heads to the Apollo Beach address on the victim's driver's license. As he pulls up to the house, he sees a cab drive away and a woman dragging one of those suitcases on wheels toward the front door.

"Excuse me ma'am. Are you Mrs. Holder?"

"Yes, what can I do for you?"

"I'm Sheriff Tony Maggio of the Hillsborough County Sheriff's Department. Can I come inside?"

"Sure," Miriam says, opening the door and walking into her living room, followed by the sheriff. "Did I break a law?"

"Is Fred Holder your husband?"

"Yes, did something happen to him?"

The sheriff pauses for a moment. "I'm afraid I have some bad news. Your husband was found stabbed to death this morning at the Lutz Motel."

Miriam slumps into a chair. "What? Who? What happened?"

"We're not sure, yet. Is there anyone I can call? Someone to stay with you for a while."

"Not really. We don't have children. I'm an only child. He has one brother who we haven't heard from in years. It's always been just Fred and me. And now it's just me." Miriam breaks down, crying.

"What was he doing at the motel?"

"He's a plumber. He was meeting with a general contractor to complete negotiations on a job."

190

"Why was he staying at a motel. Lutz is maybe forty-five minutes from here."

"When there's no traffic. He likes to get a good night's sleep and not have to fight rush hour before important meetings."

"I have to ask. Where were you on Tuesday and Wednesday?"

"I was in Charlotte, on a business trip. I work for Hillsborough County, showing various agencies how to utilize technology. All this week I was there, meeting with representatives of Conner-McGill Publishing Company. They have a software application called CompuHist. The Board of Education will be adapting this package to help teach history. Do you want the names of the people I met with?"

"Yes, please."

"You don't think I killed Fred, do you? I watch enough cop shows on TV to know that the wife is always the first suspect in cases like this. I loved Fred. I would never hurt him. Here, I can show you my hotel receipts and I had dinner on all three days with Conner-McGill executives."

"Do you know anyone who would want to hurt him?"

"No one specific. He didn't tell me much about his business, but I know he deals with some pretty rough characters. I've heard him on the phone yelling at some of these people. I think one threatened him about a week ago."

"Do you know who?"

"I don't."

"Does he keep his business records on his computer?"

"I think he does."

"Do you mind if I take it?"

"Sure, if you think it will help."

"Thanks."

"I want you to catch the bastard who did this. Is there anything else you need?"

"Not for now, ma'am. I'll be in touch. Are you sure there's no one I can call?"

"No one."

The sheriff is about to enter his car when two people approach him.

"Officer, is everything OK?" The woman appears to be in her mid-fifties, slim, attractive, with white hair and wearing a tee shirt and shorts that accentuates her femininity. "I'm Christine Lowell. This is my husband, Edgar. We live just across the street. Did something happen to Miriam?"

"No, Miriam is fine," the sheriff says. "It's Fred."

"What happened to him?"

"I'm afraid he was killed."

Was it one of his whores?" Christine asks. "Miriam pretends she doesn't know, but she knows. He goes off on those business trips and stays at those crummy motels. He can afford to stay at a good place, like a Marriott or Sheraton, but no, he stays somewhere where he can pick up some prostitute and no one will notice."

"So, you think she knew about his fooling around?"

"I think so. I work in a doctor's office. I shouldn't tell you this, what with doctor/patient confidentiality, but if it will help find who killed Fred— anyway, I know she once had a test for one of those venereal diseases."

"Chris, that's none of our business," Edgar comments.

"It could help the sheriff, dear," Christine replies. "Why else would she have herself checked if she didn't think she caught something from Fred, unless— oh no, at her age, do you think she may be fooling around. She does travel a lot, you know."

"Can you tell me anything else about Mr. and Mrs. Holder?" the sheriff inquires.

"From the way she talks at our Women's Club, he was tight with money. He had a large inheritance when his parents died, and his plumbing business is doing well."

"Real well," Edgar responds. "How else could he afford the boat he bought?"

"And he insisted they keep their money separate," Christine continues. "All she has is her income from her job, no inheritance. He bought whatever he wanted, like that boat, but gave her just enough to run the household, you know, buy stuff like food. And she has to pay for half the mortgage from her salary."

"So, he had her on an allowance," Edgar says. "What's wrong with that? It is— was his money you know."

"He wouldn't even allow her to hire a maid to clean once or twice a month," Christine notes.

"I don't see why you women need a maid," Edgar injects. "Our houses aren't that big. You all have plenty of time to keep it clean."

Christine glares at her husband. "They had a big fight before she went to some knitting convention. He didn't want her to go, said it cost too much. When she insisted, he asked why she booked a room at a Hilton. Why couldn't she stay somewhere less expensive? She refused to switch hotels. Mr. Holder stormed out of the house the night of their fight and didn't return for two days. He was a real cheapskate. Last year he told her he was going to buy her a whole new outfit, including jewelry, for our community New Year's Eve Party. And what did he do? He got everything at a thrift shop."

"So what? Those places have good stuff. I bought that sports jacket I wore to your sister's birthday party there."

Christine puts her hands on her hips and shakes her head. "And you looked real GQ. Anyway, she refused to go to the party and returned the stuff the next time the shop was open. One thing he did do for her, she told us. He paid for her to buy a gun and take lessons on how to use it."

"She owns a gun?" the sheriff inquires.

Emanuel

"Yup," Christine replies, "He said she needs it when she travels locally. At first, she didn't want it but, after a while, she gave in. She's often in restaurant and hotel parking lots after dark. I went with her to a shooting range once. She's a pretty good shot."

"Women should never be out alone after dark," Edgar says. "They need a guy to protect them."

"Seems like Miriam was real talkative at your Women's Club," the sheriff notes.

"We all are. It helps us unburden ourselves and we don't have to pay a therapist."

"Well, thank you both," the sheriff says, noting everything the Lowells told him in his notebook. The sheriff's professor friend has been trying to get him to take notes on a tablet, but he still prefers an old-fashioned pad and pen.

* * *

Hey, this stuff ain't bad," James says, "in fact, it's quite good."

The *Tech Squad* stands around the snack table, partaking of Judy's sandwiches and snacks.

"See, I told you," Judy replies. "I was skeptical three months ago when my parents decided they wanted to go vegan. They said I could opt out, and I thought about it, but that would mean I'd have to prepare my own meals. I decided to join them. I didn't like it at first, but I'm getting used to it."

Judy had made sandwiches with veggie turkey slices and vegan rye bread, and added sweet and spicy chili, tortilla chips, granola bars, and peanut butter cookies.

My students settle in at their computer terminals.

"Have you been able to come up with any new evidence about Mr. Powell's death, sheriff?" Kayla asks.

"We haven't, but we now have a second murder with the same problem. The wife appears to be the only one with a motive, but she has an iron-clad alibi."

194

"Someone else in Sun Coast Shores?" Alex inquires. "You better be careful, Doc. Next, they'll be after you."

"No," Tony replies, "this case is from Lutz. A week ago, a man who we've identified as Fred Holder was stabbed to death in some fleabag motel. The ME's report says the first wound killed him. The others occurred after he was dead.

"We've interviewed Mrs. Holder, who was in Charlotte on a business trip when her husband died. We've confirmed her alibi. We've also talked with her neighbors. From what they tell us, Mr. Holder controlled their finances. He spent lavishly on things for himself but not on anything she wanted. Their next-door neighbor," Tony flipped through his notebook, "a Mrs. Lowell, told us that the Holders had a big fight when Mrs. Holder attended some knitting conference. At first, he didn't want her to go. When she insisted, he demanded that she stay at some cheap motel to save money. She refused. Mrs. Lowell said that Mr. Holder stormed out of the house the night of their fight and didn't return for two days. We checked Holder's phone records and computer but came up blank."

"Was there any trace evidence?" James asks.

"Plenty," Tony replies. "There were hairs and blood all over the place, but none that matches Mrs. Holder. He was killed in a motel room, so we'd expect to find traces of people, but none that helps us with the case."

"Could she have paid a hit man?" Kayla asks.

"It's possible, but her financial records don't show any unusual transactions. If she paid someone, we can't find it."

"OK, class," I say. "Where do you think we should start?" I know the answer, but I want to see if they do.

"Online presence," Alex and Kayla say almost simultaneously.

"Correct. Now go at it."

Emanuel

My students attack their keyboards.

After about five minutes Kayla announces, "Mrs. Holder joined the KnitzyKnews blog. It looks like she signed up at about the time she attended a knitting conference."

"She also spends time on Florida state education web sites and looks for information about technology used in schools," Alex notes.

"That's probably because she works for the state and shows teachers and administrators how to use technology in the classroom," Tony replies.

"Mr. Holder looks at plumbing web sites," Diego chimes in. "Looks like a lot of boring stuff."

"He's a plumber," Tony responds.

"He also spends time on porno sites," James says.

"Just like a man," Adiva replies.

The Tech squad spends the remainder of the workshop trying to find something that would help them either show that Mrs. Holder killed her husband, or to identify someone else. I can see the frustration on their faces.

"You know, team," I say, "the cops don't solve every case, at least not immediately. This isn't TV or the movies. It's the real world. Let the sheriff dig some more into the case. We'll take it up again at next week's workshop." I can see the dejected looks on everyone's face as they leave the room. They're used to solving cases, and now they have two they can't seem to crack.

* * *

After the workshop, Kayla heads to the gym for basketball practice.

"Hey, Point," Kayla says as she enters the dressing room and high fives her best friend, Donna Jeffreys, the team's Point Guard.

"Back at you, Forward," Donna replies.

"I heard the good news, a full scholarship to the University of North Carolina in the fall. We'll miss you."

"And I'll miss you guys. I'll be home when we have school breaks, so let's get together, then. Don't be a stranger."

"I won—." Kayla stops in the middle of her response. "Point, you go ahead to practice. I'll meet you out there in five minutes. I've got something to do first."

"Don't be too long. Coach hates it when we're late."

Donna walks toward the court and Kayla grabs her phone from her locker. "Sheriff, I may have the answer to both of those murders."

* * *

The Sun Coast Shores Tuesday evening knitting group has just finished dessert and is about to move to the Arts and Crafts Room. As the women pass through the Clubhouse lobby, they see two uniformed police officers enter the front door. Sarah recognizes them as Sheriff Tony Maggio and Deputy Daniel Boudreau. The two men approach Sarah.

"Sarah Powell," the Sheriff says, "you're under arrest."

"For what!"

"The murder of Fred Holder."

* * *

For a month after Fred's death, neighbors come to show their respect. Miriam does her best to appear the grieved widow. Once the condolence calls stop, she's ready to set the wheels in motion to start her new life. She donates his clothing and other possessions to Goodwill. She considers keeping his golf clubs as a memento but decides against it. One of his old golfing buddies is happy to take it off her hands.

Miriam is sitting in her lounge chair, knitting, when she hears the doorbell ring. She opens the door to see the sheriff and deputy who had talked to her three or four times after Fred was killed. She knows they suspect her. They always suspect the spouse, but she has an iron clad alibi.

197

Emanuel

"Miriam Holder," the Sheriff says, "you're under arrest for the murder of Richard Powell."

* * *

Three days after the most recent workshop, Diego enters my office. "I hear Kayla broke both cases wide open."

"She did, and she'll show us how at Friday's workshop."

"Great, and the team has one request. We enjoy everyone bringing snacks, but this week we'd like something all of us can relate to, regardless of what we get at home."

* * *

As I approach the Sheriff's Department Technology Center on Friday afternoon, I hold the door open for a man carrying three boxes. I guess, regardless of a person's family background, everyone likes pizza. When I go to the snack table, I even see one of them has a mushroom topping. These kids are fearless.

"Kayla saved us," Diego says, putting his arm around his classmate and, switching to his Mohammed Ali voice, "we're still the greatest."

I motion to Kayla. "The podium's yours, young lady. Show the rest of us how you solved these cases."

Kayla points to Judy. "Remember, in our Twentieth Century American Literature class, we were asked to do a book report."

"Yeah, I chose *Gentleman's Agreement*."

"And do you remember my book?"

"I think it was something about a train."

"It's called *Strangers on a Train*. It's about two men who meet on a train, one who wants his father killed, and the other, his wife. The man who wants his father dead murders the other guy's wife. Once she's gone, the second man kills the first man's father. The man whose wife was murdered has an alibi for when she died, and the guy

198

whose father dies has an alibi for when he was killed. Exactly like our cases. We have two women who have reasons to want their husbands killed and both have alibis for when their spouses died. Earlier this week I sat down with the sheriff and the Doc and we found some interesting stuff."

Kayla displays both widows' bank statements, with a transaction highlighted on each document. "This shows where they first met. They both attended a knitting conference in Atlanta and stayed at the same hotel. We found no indication that the women knew each other prior to their meeting in Atlanta, so we assume they met there and hatched their plan.

"Digging further, we learned that Mrs. Powell is a surgical nurse. Mr. Holder was stabbed. The ME's report says the first wound killed him. The others occurred after he was dead. As a surgical nurse, Mrs. Powell would know exactly where to thrust the knife to kill him."

Kayla adds Sarah Powell's picture to the display. "The sheriff got warrants for the community association's fitness center logs. Mrs. Powell spends a lot of time at the gym and we see, from her picture, she's in excellent physical condition."

Kayla displays a copy of Fred Holder's credit card receipts. "Mr. Holder had a good deal to drink the night he was killed. Mrs. Powell's strength and Mr. Holder's weakened condition due to alcohol made it easy for Mrs. Powell to confront and stab him."

"But why did Mrs. Powell want her husband dead?" Adiva asks.

"I can answer that," Tony replies. "We learned from Mrs. Powell's doctor that he had a degenerative hip condition. One of her neighbors was very open with Deputy Boudreau about how she spent most of her time taking care of her husband. She knew his condition

Emanuel

wouldn't improve. She would be a care giver for the rest of her life."

"Once we suspected the *Strangers on a Train* scenario," Kayla continues, "we looked to see if we could place Mrs. Holder in Sun Coast Estates the evening of Mr. Powell's murder."

"Did you find anything?" Alex asks.

"We did. There's a camera in a 7-Eleven parking lot, which is not far from where Mr. Powell was killed." Kayla displays the 7-Eleven video. "We see Mrs. Holder's car parked there from 7:00 – 8:30. One photo clearly identifies her license plate. Her GPS system also shows her making a trip to the 7-Eleven the night Mr. Powell died."

Tony points to another entry on Miriam Holder's bank statement. "Mrs. Holder spent time at a shooting range, learning to fire a pistol. We interviewed the shooting range's manager and some people who knew her there. They told us that, at first, she was reluctant to shoot, but once she got the hang of it, she became quite a marksman."

"Can you place Mrs. Powell at the crime scene the night of Mr. Holder's murder?" James asks. "Are there any surveillance cameras?"

"There aren't," Tony replies, "but Mrs. Powell's GPS system shows her going to and from the motel twice. We're assuming she went one evening but couldn't get the job done, so she returned the next night."

"OK," James asks, "how did each of them know where the other's husband would be at the time they were killed? We couldn't find any evidence that they ever communicated?"

"KnitzyKnews," Kayla replies. "Both women subscribe to that knitter's blog. I played a hunch that they may have used it to communicate. Mrs. Powell has been active on the site for almost three years. Mrs. Holder first logged on at the conference. I couldn't find any communications between the two women. Then I thought about private chat rooms. I found that Mrs. Powell and Mrs. Holder set one up, for just the two of them. When we accessed posts in this private chat room we found—," Kayla pauses a few seconds, "—nothing."

I can hear a sigh of disappointment from the class. They expected to find critical evidence there. Alex's face brightens, and he smiles. I figured he would be the first to understand, and I'm right. "But we all know that nothing disappears from cyberspace."

"Alex is right," Kayla says. "We dug into the private chat room's deleted posts. Mrs. Powell began posting immediately after the conference, letting Mrs. Holder know when Mr. Holder would be going to the first tee. She did this every evening for three weeks, until Mrs. Holder posted *I'm In.* We're assuming Mrs. Holder was telling Mrs. Powell that she would kill Mr. Powell. Mrs. Holder posted *Tonight* the evening she planned to kill Mr. Powell and *Done* after she murdered him. The *Done* post pinged off a cell tower near where Mr. Powell was killed.

"Mrs. Holder posted the date when her husband would be staying at the motel and the room number. She stated that he's usually in his room by 11:00 PM. Mrs. Powell posted *Done* when she had completed her task. Mrs. Powell's *Done* post pinged off a cell tower near the hotel where Mr. Holder was killed. The two women then erased the posts, assuming no one would find them. They were wrong."

"Did you find the knife or the gun?" Adiva asks.

"Unfortunately, no," Tony replies. "Both of their GPS systems show them driving down a dirt road leading to the Alafia River, Mrs. Powell, the night she killed Mr. Holder, and Mrs. Holder after her husband was killed. Mrs. Holder probably realized that she couldn't get rid of the gun when her husband was still alive because he might ask about it. We're assuming they threw the weapons into the flowing water. We sent divers down but found nothing. The current probably took the weapons down to the Gulf."

"It sounds like you have a lot of circumstantial evidence," Adiva responds. "Will it hold up in court?"

"Kayla, do you want to show them the coup de grâce?" Tony replies.

"The sheriff got a warrant for both women's DNA. We went back and looked at the trace evidence, and, sure enough, we found two of Mrs. Holder's hairs at the golf course, and a fabric strand containing Mrs. Powell's DNA in the motel room."

"Mrs. Holder took a big chance," Alex notes. "She killed Mr. Powell first. How did she know that Mrs. Powell would fulfill her end of the bargain, and kill Mr. Holder? What would Mrs. Holder do, call the cops on Mrs. Powell?"

"I guess Mrs. Powell didn't want to be looking over her shoulder the rest of her life, fearing an angry woman who knows how to use a gun."

* * *

<u>Six Years Later</u>

"Thank you very much," Virginia says, "I will see you on September fifteenth." Virginia disconnects from the Skype video call to her client and immediately dials Brenda Ellison, her partner. "I got it. Please put on the calendar that I'll be away September 15 – 20. I'll be home for Jeremy's birthday on the 22nd."

Life had been good to Virginia, very good indeed. The time she spent talking with Sarah and Miriam had made her feel good about herself and had given her the incentive to start planning the next chapter in her life. Two days after she completed her assignment at that knitting conference, she applied to Fulton County Community College and registered to study Business Administration. She went on to earn a bachelor's degree from the University of Georgia. During her junior year she met Brenda. They married immediately after graduation.

It was Brenda who came up with the idea for her business. "You keep saying how your most recognizable skill is killing people," she had said. "That's not true. Your most recognizable skill is using weapons properly. Why not start a business offering weapons training?" That's exactly what Virginia did. She got seed money from two Small Business Administration programs, one which helps women start a business and the other targeted to veterans. She had gotten the idea about applying for government funding that day, six years ago, when she met those two women in the park. One of them, she thinks it was Miriam, told her that she helps school districts apply for education loans and grants. She suggested that Virginia look into government assistance to help small business owners.

Initially, she was the face of the company and Brenda managed the office. Once they began earning a profit, they decided to adopt Jeremy, and a year later, Keven. Brenda was happy to become a stay-at-home mom, and Virginia could afford to hire two people to man the office and a Marine veteran as a second trainer.

She often thought about the two women she met at that conference. She was sorry she hadn't gotten their contact information. She would like to thank them. She'd like to know what had happened to them. She wondered if either of them had ever read the book that appeared to fascinate them that day in the park, *Strangers on a Train*.

Made in the USA
Columbia, SC
07 November 2024

45560729R00124